A Christmas Promise

A Christmas Promise

A Novel

Anne Perry

BALLANTINE BOOKS · NEW YORK

Copyright © 2009 by Anne Perry

Published in the United States by Ballantine Books, an imprint of The Random House Publishing Group, a division of Random House, Inc., New York.

BALLANTINE and colophon are registered trademarks of Random House, Inc.

LIBRARY OF CONGRESS CATALOGING-IN-PUBLICATION DATA
Perry, Anne.
A Christmas promise : a novel / Anne Perry. —1st ed.
p. cm.
ISBN 978-0-345-51066-2 (alk. paper)
1. Poor children—England—London—Fiction.   2. City and town life—England—London—Fiction.   3. East End (London, England)—Fiction.   4. Christmas stories.   I. Title.
PR6066.E693C473 2009b
823'.914—dc22   2009035431

Printed in the United States of America on acid-free paper

www.ballantinebooks.com

2 4 6 8 9 7 5 3 1

FIRST EDITION

Text design by Julie Schroeder

A Christmas Promise

$\mathcal{T}$HE WEEK BEFORE CHRISTMAS, THE SMELL and taste of it were in the air, a kind of excitement, an urgency about everything. Geese and rabbits hung outside butchers' shops, and there were little pieces of holly on some people's doors. Postmen were extra busy. The streets were still gray, the wind still hard and cold, the rain turning to sleet, but it wouldn't have seemed right if it had been different.

Gracie Phipps was on an errand for her gran to get a tuppence worth of potatoes to go with the leftovers of cabbage and onion, so Gran could make bubble and squeak for supper. Spike and Finn would pretty well eat anything they could fit into their mouths, but they liked this especially. Better with a slice of sausage, of course, but there was no money for that now. Everything was being saved for Christmas.

Gracie walked a little faster into the wind, pulling her shawl tighter around her. She had the potatoes in a string bag, along with half a cabbage. She saw the girl standing by the candle makers, on the corner of Heneage Street and Brick Lane, her reddish fair hair blowing about and her arms hugged around her as if she were freezing. She looked to be about eight, five years younger than Gracie, and as skinny as an eel. She had to be lost. She didn't belong there, or on Chicksand Street—one over. Gracie had lived on these streets ever since she had come to London from the country, when her mother had died six years before, in 1877. She knew everyone.

"Are yer lorst?" she asked as she reached the child. "This is 'Eneage Street. Where d'yer come from?"

The girl looked at her with wide gray eyes, blinking fiercely in an attempt to stop the tears from brimming over onto her cheeks. "Thrawl Street," she answered. That was two streets over to the west and on the other side of Brick Lane, out of the neighborhood altogether.

"It's that way." Gracie pointed.

"I know where it is," the girl replied, not making any effort to move. "Me uncle Alf's bin killed, an' Charlie's gorn. I gotta find 'im, cos 'e'll be cold an' 'ungry, an' mebbe scared." Her eyes brimmed over, and she wiped her sleeve across her face and sniffed. "'Ave yer seen a donkey as yer don't know? 'E's gray, wi' brown eyes, an' a sort o' pale bit round the end of 'is nose." She looked at Gracie with sudden, intense hope. "'E's about this 'igh." She indicated, reaching upward with a small, dirty hand.

Gracie would have liked to help, but she had seen no animals at all, except for the coal man's horse at the end of the street, and a couple of stray dogs. Even hansom cabs didn't often come to this part of the East End. Commercial Street, or

Whitechapel Road, maybe, on their way to some-where else. She looked at the child's eager face and felt her heart sink. "Wot's yer name?" she asked.

"Minnie Maude Mudway," the child replied. "But I in't lorst. I'm lookin' fer Charlie. 'E's the one wot's lorst, an' summink might 'ave 'appened to 'im. I told yer, me uncle Alf's bin killed. Yesterday it were, an' Charlie's gorn. 'E'd 'ave come 'ome if 'e could. 'E must be cold an' 'ungry, an' 'e dunno where 'e is."

Gracie was exasperated. The whole story made no sense. Why would Minnie Maude be worrying about a donkey that had wandered off, if her uncle had really been killed? And yet she couldn't just leave the girl there standing on the corner in the wind. It would be dark very soon. It was after three already, and going to rain. "Yer got a ma?" Gracie asked.

"No," Minnie Maude answered. "I got an aunt Bertha, but she says as Charlie don't matter. Don-keys is donkeys."

"Well, if yer uncle got killed, maybe she don't care that much about donkeys right now." Gracie tried to sound reasonable. "Wot's gonna 'appen to 'er, wif 'im gone? Yer gotta think as she might be scared an' all."

Minnie Maude blinked. "Uncle Alf di'n't matter to 'er like that," she explained. " 'E were me pa's bruvver." She sniffed harder. "Uncle Alf told good stories. 'E'd bin ter places, an' 'e saw things better than most folk. Saw them fer real, wot they meant inside, not just wot's plain. 'E used ter make me laugh."

Gracie felt a sudden, sharp sense of the girl's loss. Maybe it was Uncle Alf she was really look- ing for, and Charlie was just an excuse, a kind of sideways way of seeing it, until she could bear to look at it straight. There was something very spe- cial about people who made you laugh. "I'm sorry," she said gently. It had been a little while before she had really said to herself that her mother wasn't ever coming back.

7

"'E were killed," Minnie Maude repeated. "Yest'day."

"Then yer'd best go 'ome," Gracie pointed out. "Yer aunt'll be wond'rin' wot 'appened to yer. Mebbe Charlie's already got 'ome 'isself."

Minnie Maude looked miserable and defiant, shivering in the wind and almost at the end of her strength. "No 'e won't. If 'e knew 'ow ter come 'ome 'e'd a bin there last night. 'E's cold an' scared, an' all by 'isself. An' no one but 'im an' me knows as Uncle Alf were done in. Aunt Bertha says as 'e fell off an' 'it 'is 'ead, broke 'is neck most like. An' Stan says it don't matter anyway, cos dead is dead jus' the same, an' we gotta bury 'im decent, an' get on wi' things. Ain't no time ter sit around. Stan drives an 'ansom, 'e goes all over the place, but 'e don't know as much as Uncle Alf did. 'E could fall over summink wifout seein' it proper. 'E sees wot it is, like Uncle Alf said, but 'e don't never see wot it could be! 'E di'n't see as donkeys can be as good as a proper 'orse."

Not for a hansom cab, Gracie thought. Who ever saw a hansom with a donkey in the shafts? But she didn't say so.

"An' Aunt Bertha di'n't 'old wif animals," Minnie Maude finished. " 'Ceptin' cats, cos they get the mice." She gulped and wiped her nose on her sleeve again. "So will yer 'elp me look for Charlie, please?"

Gracie felt useless. Why couldn't she have come a little earlier, when her gran had first told her to? Then she wouldn't even have been here for this child to ask her for something completely impossible. She felt sad and guilty, but there was no possible way she could go off around the wet winter streets in the dark, looking for donkeys. She had to get home with the potatoes so her gran could make supper for them, and the two hungry little boys Gran's son had left when he'd died. They were nearly old enough to get out and earn their own way, but right now they were still a considerable responsibility, especially with Gracie's gran earning only what she could doing laundry every hour she was awake, and a few when she hardly was. Gracie helped with errands. She always seemed to be running around fetching or carrying something, cleaning, sweeping, scrubbing. But very soon she would have to go to the factory like other girls, as soon as Spike and Finn didn't need watching.

"I can't," she said quietly. "I gotta go 'ome with the taters, or them kids'll start eatin' the chairs. Then I gotta 'elp me gran." She wanted to apologize, but what was the point? The answer was still no.

Minnie Maude nodded, her mouth tightening a little. She breathed in and out deeply, steadying herself. "'S all right. I'll look fer Charlie meself." She sniffed and turned away to walk home. The sky was darkening and the first spots of rain were heavy in the wind, hard and cold.

When Gracie pushed the back door open to their lodgings in Heneage Street, her grandmother was standing with a basin of water ready to wash and peel the potatoes. She looked worn-out from spending all day up to her elbows in hot water, caustic, and lye, heaving other people's wet linen from one sink to another, shoulders aching, back so sore she could hardly touch it. Then she would have to lift the linen all again to wind it through the mangles that would squeeze the water out, and there would be some chance of getting it dry so it could be returned, and paid for. There was always need for money: rent, food, boots, a few sticks and a little coal to put on the fire, and of course Christmas.

Gracie hardly grew out of anything. It seemed as if she had stopped at four feet eleven, and worn-out pieces could always be patched. But Spike and Finn were bigger every time you looked at them, and considering how much they ate, perhaps no one should have been surprised.

The food was good, and every scrap disappeared, even though they were being careful and saving any treats for Christmas. Spike and Finn bickered a bit, as usual, then went off to bed obediently enough at about seven. There wasn't a clock, but if you thought about it, and you were used to the sounds of the street outside, footsteps coming and going, the voices of those you knew, then you had a good idea of time.

They had two rooms, which wasn't bad, considering. There was the kitchen, with a tin bowl for washing; the stove, to cook and keep warm; and the table and three chairs and a stool. And there was the bench for chopping, ironing, and baking now and then. There was a drain outside the back door, a well at the end of the street, and a privy at the bottom of the yard. In the other small room, Gracie and her gran had beds on one side, and on the other they had built a sort of bed for the boys. They lay in it, one at each end.

But Gracie did not sleep well, in spite of being very nearly warm enough. She could not forget Minnie Maude Mudway, standing on the street corner in the dusk, grieving for loneliness, death, a donkey who might or might not be lost. All night it troubled her, and she woke to the bleak, icy morning still miserable.

She got up quickly, without disturbing her gran, who needed every moment of sleep she could find. Gracie pulled on her clothes immediately. The air was as cold as stone on her skin. There was ice on the inside of the windows as well as on the outside.

She tiptoed out into the kitchen, put on her boots, and buttoned them up. Then she started to rake out the dead ashes from the kitchen stove and relight it so she could heat a pan of water and make porridge for breakfast. That was a luxury not everyone had, and she tasted it with pleasure every time.

Spike and Finn came in before daylight, although there was a paling of the sky above the rooftops. They were full of good spirits, planning mischief, and glad enough to eat anything they were given: porridge, a heel of bread, and a smear of dripping. By half past eight they were off on errands for the woman at the corner shop, and Gran, fortified by a cup of tea, insisting it was enough, went on her way back to the laundry.

Gracie busied herself with housework, washing dishes, sweeping, and dusting, putting out slops and fetching more water from the well at the end of the street. It was cold outside, with a rime of ice on the cobbles and a hard east wind promising sleet.

By nine o'clock she could not bear her conscience anymore. She put on her heaviest shawl, gray-brown cloth and very thick, and went outside into the street again and down to the corner to look for Minnie Maude.

London was an enormous cluster of villages all running into one another, some rich, some poor, none worse than Flower and Dean Walk, which was filled with rotting tenements, sometimes

eight or ten people to a room. It was full of prosti-
tutes, thieves, magsmen, cracksmen, star-glazers,
snotter-haulers, fogle-hunters, and pickpockets of
every kind.

Oddly enough, the boundaries remained. Each
village had its own identity and loyalties, its hier-
archies of importance and rules of behavior, its
racial and religious mixtures. Just the other side of
Commercial Street it was Jewish, mostly Russians
and Poles. In the other direction was Whitechapel.
Thrawl Street, where Minnie Maude said she
lived, was beyond Gracie's area. Only something as
ignorant as a donkey would wander from one village to another as if there were no barriers, just because you could not see them. Charlie could hardly
be blamed, poor creature, but Minnie Maude knew,
and of course Gracie did even more so.

At the corner the wind was harder. It sliced
down the open street, whining in the eaves of the
taller buildings, their brick defaced with age,

weathering, and neglect. Water stains from broken guttering streaked black, and she knew they would smell of mold inside, like dirty socks.

The soles of her boots slipped on the ice, and her feet were so cold she could not feel her toes anymore.

The next street over was busy with people, men going to work at the lumberyard or the coal merchant, girls going to the match factory a little farther up. One passed her, and Gracie saw for a moment the lopsided disfigurement of her face, known as "phossie-jaw," caused by the phosphorus in the match heads. An old woman was bent over, carrying a bundle of laundry. Two others shared a joke, laughing loudly. There was a peddler on the opposite corner with a tray of sandwiches, and a man in a voluminous coat slouched by.

A brewer's dray passed, horses lifting their great feet proudly and clattering them on the stones, harnesses gleaming even in the washed-out winter light. Nothing more beautiful than a horse, strong and gentle, its huge feet with hair like silk skirts around them.

A hawker came a few yards behind, pushing a barrow full of vegetables, pearly buttons on his coat. He was whistling a tune, and Gracie recognized it as a Christmas carol. The words were something about merry gentlemen.

She walked quickly to get out of the wind; it would be more sheltered once she was around the corner. She knew what street she was looking for. She could remember the name, but she could not read the signs. She was going to have to ask someone, and she hated that. It took away all her independence and made her feel foolish. At least someone would know Minnie Maude, especially since there had just been a death in the family.

She was regarded with some suspicion, but five minutes later she stood on the narrow pavement outside a grimy brick-fronted house whose colorless wooden door was shut fast against the ice-laden wind.

Until this moment Gracie had not thought of what she was going to say to explain her presence. She could hardly tell them that she had come to help Minnie Maude find Charlie, because if she were really a good person, she would have offered to do that yesterday. Going home to tea sounded like an excuse. And anyway, Aunt Bertha had already said that, as far as she was concerned, it didn't matter, and whatever Minnie Maude thought of it, Aunt Bertha seemed reasonable enough. The poor woman was bereaved, and probably beside herself with worry as to how they were going to manage without a money-earning member of the family. There was a funeral to pay for, never mind looking for daft donkeys that had wandered off. Except that he might be worth a few shillings if they sold him?

Probably they already had, and just didn't want to tell Minnie Maude. She was too young to understand some of the realities of life. That was probably it. Better to tell her, though. Then she would stop worrying that he was lost and scared and out in the rain by himself.

Gracie was still standing uselessly on the cobbles, shifting from one foot to the other and shaking with cold, when the door opened and a large man with a barrel chest and bowlegs came out, banging his hands together as if they were already numb.

"Eh, mister!" Gracie stepped forward into his path. "Is this where Minnie Maude lives?"

He looked startled. "I in't seen you 'ere before! 'Oo are yer?" he demanded.

"I in't bin 'ere before," she said reasonably. "That's 'ow I dunno if this is where she lives."

He looked her up and down, all four feet eleven inches of her, from the top of her shawl to her pale, clever little face, down to her bony body and her worn-out boots with buttons missing. "Wot d'yer want wif our Minnie Maude, then?" he asked suspiciously.

Gracie said the first thing that came into her

mind. "Got an errand for 'er. Worf tuppence, if she does it right. Can't do it all meself," she added, in case it sounded too good to be true.

"I'll get 'er for yer," he said instantly, turning on his heel and going back into the house. A moment later he returned with Minnie Maude behind him. "There y'are," he said, and pushed her forward. "Make yerself useful, then," he prompted, as if she might be reluctant.

Minnie Maude's wide eyes regarded Gracie with wonder and gratitude entirely inappropriate to the offer of a twopenny job, which might even last all day. Still, perhaps when you were eight, tuppence was a lot. Gracie was thirteen, and it was more than she actually had, but she had needed to make the offer good in order to be certain that it would be carried inside, and that Minnie Maude would be allowed to accept. She would deal with finding the tuppence later.

"Well, c'mon, then!" Gracie said aloud, grasping Minnie Maude's arm and half-pulling her away from the bowlegged man and striding along the street as fast as she dared on the ice.

"Yer gonna 'elp me find Charlie?" Minnie Maude asked breathlessly, slipping and struggling to keep up with her.

It was a little too late to justify her answer now. "Yeah," Gracie conceded. "I 'spec it won't take long. Someb'dy'll 'ave seen 'im. Mebbe 'e got a fright an' ran off. 'E'll get 'isself 'ome by an' by. Wot 'appened ter yer uncle Alf, anyway?" She slowed down a little bit now that they were round the corner and back in Brick Lane again.

"Dunno," Minnie Maude said unhappily. "They found 'im in Richard Street, in Mile End, lyin' in the road wi' the back of 'is 'ead stove in, an' cuts an' bangs all over 'im. They said as 'e must 'ave fell off 'is cart. But Charlie'd never 'ave gorn an' left 'im like that. Couldn't've, even if 'e'd wanted to, bein' as 'e were tied inter the shafts."

"W'ere's the cart, then?" Gracie asked practically.

21

"That's it!" Minnie Maude exclaimed, stopping abruptly. "It's not there! That's 'ow else I know 'e were done in. It's gorn."

Gracie shook her head, stopping beside her. " 'Oo'd a done 'im in? Wot's in the cart, then? Milk? Coal? Taters?" She was beginning to feel more and more as if Minnie Maude were in her own world of loss and grief more than in the real one. " 'Oo's gonna do in someone fer a cartload o' taters? 'E must a died natural, an' fell off, poor thing. Then some rotten bastard stole 'is cart, taters an' all, an' Charlie wif 'em. But 'owever rotten they are," she added hastily, "they'll look after Charlie, because 'e's worf summink. Donkeys are useful."

"It weren't milk," Minnie Maude said, easing her pace to keep in step. " 'E were a rag an' bone man, an' sometimes 'e 'ad real beautiful things, treasures. It could a bin anyfink." She left the possibilities dangling in the air.

Gracie looked sideways at her. She was about

three inches shorter than Gracie, and just as thin. Her small face had a dusting of freckles across the nose, and at the moment it was pinched with worry. Gracie felt a strong stab of pity for her.

" 'E'll mebbe come back by 'isself," she said as encouragingly as she could. "Unless 'e's in a nice stable somewhere, an' can't get out. I 'spec someone nicked the cart, cos there were some good stuff in it. But donkeys in't daft." She had never actually known a donkey, but she knew the coal man's horse, and it was intelligent enough. It could always find a carrot top, whatever pocket you put it in.

Minnie Maude forced a smile. "Course," she said bravely. "We just gotta ask, afore 'e gets so lorst an' can't find 'is way back. Actual, I dunno 'ow far 'e's ever bin. More 'n I 'ave, prob'ly."

"Well, we'd best get started, then." Gracie surrendered her common sense to a moment's weakness of sympathy. Minnie Maude was a stubborn little article, and daft as a brush with it. Who knew what would happen to her if she was left on her own? Gracie would give it an hour or two. She could spare that much. Maybe Charlie would come back himself by then.

"Fank yer," Minnie Maude acknowledged. "Where we gonna start?" She looked at Gracie hopefully.

Gracie's mind raced for an answer. " 'Oo found yer uncle Alf, then?"

"Jimmy Quick," Minnie Maude replied immediately. " 'E's a lyin' git an' all, but that's prob'ly true, cos 'e 'ad ter get 'elp."

"Then we'll go an' find Jimmy Quick an' ask 'im," Gracie said firmly. "If 'e tells us exact, mebbe takes us there, we can ask folks, an' p'raps someone saw Charlie. Where'd we look fer 'im?"

"In the street." Minnie Maude squinted up at the leaden winter sky, apparently judging the time. "Mebbe Church Lane, be now. Or mebbe 'e in't started yet, an' 'e's still at 'ome in Angel Alley."

"Started wot?"

" 'Is way round. 'E's a rag an' bone man, too. That's 'ow come 'e found Uncle Alf."

"Rag an' bone men don't do the same round as each other," Gracie pointed out. "It don't make no sense. There'd be nuffink left." She was as patient as she could be. Minnie Maude was only eight, but she should have been able to work that out.

"I tol' yer 'e were a lyin' git," Minnie Maude replied, unperturbed.

"Well, we better find 'im anyway." Gracie had no better idea. "Which way d'we go?"

"That way." Minnie Maude pointed after a minute's hesitation, in which she swiveled around slowly, facing each direction in turn. She set off confidently, marching across the cobbles, her feet clattering on the ice and her heart in her mouth. Gracie caught up with her, hoping to heaven that they would not both get as lost as Charlie.

They crossed Wentworth Street away from the places she knew, and had left them behind in a few hundred yards. Now all the streets looked frighteningly the same, narrow and uneven. Here and there cobbles were broken or missing, gutters swollen with the previous night's rain and the refuse from unknown numbers of houses. Alleys threaded off to either side, some little more than the width of a man's outstretched arms, the house eaves almost meeting overhead. The strip of sky above was no more than a jagged crack. Gutters dripped, and most hung with ice. Some of the blackened chimneys belched smoke.

Everyone was busy on errands of one sort or another, pushing carts of vegetables, bales of cloth, kegs of ale—rickety wheels catching the curbs. Children shouted, peddlers called their wares, and patterers rehearsed the latest news and gossip in singsong voices, making up colloquial rhymes. Women quarreled; several dogs ran around barking.

At the end of the next road was the Whitechapel High Street, a wide thoroughfare with hansom cabs bowling along at a brisk clip, cabbies riding high on the boxes. There was even a gentleman's carriage with a matched pair of bay horses with brass on their harness and a beautiful pattern on the carriage door.

"We gone too far," Minnie Maude said. "Angel Alley's back that way." She started along the High Street, then suddenly turned into one of the alleys again, and after a further hundred yards or so, she turned into a ramshackle yard with a sign at the entrance.

"I fink this is it," she said, peering at the letters. But looking at her face all screwed up in uncertainty, Gracie knew perfectly well that she was only guessing.

Minnie Maude took a deep breath and walked in. Gracie followed. She couldn't let her go in alone.

A lean man with straight black hair came out of one of the sheds.

"There's nothing 'ere fer kids," he said with a slight lisp. He waved his hands. "Orff wif yer!"

"Ye're Jimmy Quick?" Minnie Maude pulled herself up very straight.

" 'Oo are you, then?" he said, puzzled.

"Minnie Maude Mudway," she replied. "It were me uncle Alf as yer found in the street." She hesitated. "An' this is me friend," she added.

"Gracie Phipps," Gracie said.

"We're lookin' fer Charlie," Minnie Maude went on.

Jimmy Quick frowned at them. "I dunno no Charlie."

" 'E's a donkey," Gracie explained. Someone needed to talk a little sense. " 'E got lost, along wif Uncle Alf's cart, an' everyfink wot was in it." She glanced around the yard and saw three old bicycles whose wheels had missing spokes, several odd boots and shoes, kettles, pieces of china and pottery, some of it so beautiful she stared at it in amazement. There were old fire irons, a poker with a brass handle, ornaments, pots and pans, pieces of carpet, a cabin trunk with no hinges, unwanted books and pictures, all the things a rag and bone man collects, in with the actual rags or bones for glue.

Minnie Maude stood still, ignoring the scattered takings around her, just staring solemnly at Jimmy Quick. " 'Ow'd yer find 'im, then?"

Jimmy seemed to consider evading the question, then changed his mind. " 'E were jus' lyin' there in the road," he said sadly. "Like 'e fell off, 'cept o' course 'e'd never 'ave done that, if 'e'd bin alive. I've seen Alf as tight as a newt, an' 'e didn't miss a step, never mind fell. 'E knew 'ow ter wedge 'isself, like, so 'e wouldn't—not even if 'e were asleep." He shook his head. "Reckon as 'ow 'e must 'ave just died all of a sudden. Bin took, as it were. Visitation o' God."

"No 'e weren't," Minnie Maude contradicted him. "If 'e 'ad bin, Charlie'd 'ave brought 'im 'ome. An' wot were 'e doin' way out 'ere anyway? This in't 'is patch." She sniffed fiercely as if on the edge of tears. "Someone's done 'im in."

"Yer talkin' daft," Jimmy said dismissively, but his face was very pink. " 'Oo'd wanter 'urt Alf?" He looked uncomfortable, not quite meeting Minnie Maude's eyes. Gracie wondered if it was embarrassment because he did not know how to comfort her, or something uglier that he was trying not to say.

Gracie interrupted at last. "It in't daft," she told him. "Wot 'appened ter Charlie, an' the cart? 'E di'n't go 'ome."

Now Jimmy Quick was deeply unhappy. "I dunno. Yer sure the cart's not at yer aunt Bertha's?" he asked Minnie Maude.

She looked at him witheringly. "Course it in't. Charlie might get lorst, cos this in't where 'e usually comes. So why was 'e 'ere? Even if Uncle Alf died an' fell off, which 'e wouldn't 'ave, why'd nobody see 'im 'ceptin' you? An' 'oo took Charlie an' the cart?"

Put like that, Gracie had to agree that it didn't

sound right at all. She joined Minnie Maude in staring accusingly at Jimmy Quick.

Jimmy looked down at the ground with even greater unhappiness, and what now most certainly appeared to be guilt. "It were my fault," he admitted. "I 'ad ter go up ter Artillery Lane an' see someone, or I'd a bin in real trouble, so I asked Alf ter trade routes wi' me. 'E'd do mine, an' I'd do 'is. That way I could be where I 'ad ter, wi'out missin' an 'ole day. That's why 'e were 'ere. 'E were a good mate ter me, an' 'e died doin' me a favor."

" 'E were on yer round!" Gracie said in sudden realization of all that meant. "So if someone done 'im in, p'raps they meant it ter be you!"

"Nobody's gonna do me in!" Jimmy said with alarm, but looking at his face, paler now and a little gray around his lips, Gracie knew that the thought was sharp in his mind, and growing sharper with every minute.

She made her own expression as grim as she

could, drawing her eyebrows down and tightening her mouth, just as Gran did when she found an immovable stain in someone's best linen. "But yer jus' said as 'e were alone cos 'e were doin' yer a favor," she pointed out. "If nobody else knew that, they'd a thought as it were you sittin' in the cart!"

"I dunno," Jimmy said unhappily.

Gracie did not believe him. Her mind raced over how it could matter, picking up people's odd pieces of throwaway, or the things they might buy or sell, if they knew where. What did rag and bone men pick up, anyway? If you could pawn it for a few pence, or maybe more, you took it to the shop. She glanced at Minnie Maude, who was standing hunched up, shaking with cold, and now looking defeated.

Gracie lost her temper. "Course yer know!" she shouted at Jimmy. " 'E got done in doin' yer job, cos yer asked 'im ter. An' now the cart's gorn and Charlie's gorn, an' we're standin' 'ere freezin', an' yer sayin' as yer can't tell us wot 'e died fer!"

"Cos I dunno!" Jimmy said helplessly. He swung his arms in the air. "Come on inside an' Dora'll make yer a cup o' tea." He led the way across the yard, weaving between bicycles, cart wheels, milk churns without lids, until he came to the back door of his house. He pushed the door wide, invitingly, and they crowded in after him.

Inside the kitchen was a splendid collection of every kind of odd piece of machinery and equipment a scrap yard could acquire. Nothing matched anything else, hardly two pieces of china were from the same set, yet it was all excellent, the most delicate Gracie had ever seen, hand-painted and rimmed in gold. No two saucepans were the same either, or had lids that fitted, but all were handsome enough, even if there was little to put in them besides potatoes, onions, and cabbage, and perhaps a few bones for flavor.

In the far corner stood a magnificent mangle, with odd rollers, one white, one gray; a collection of flatirons, most of them broken; and several lanterns missing either sides or handles. Perhaps the bits and pieces might make two usable ones between them?

Mrs. Quick was standing expectantly by the stove, on which a copper kettle was gleaming in the gaslight, steam whistling out of the spout. She was an ample woman wearing a blue dress patched in a dozen places without thought for matching anything, and she wore a marvelous old velvet cape around her shoulders. It was vivid red, and apart from a burn on one side, appeared as good as new.

"Ah! So you're Bert Mudway's girl," she said to Minnie Maude with satisfaction, then turned to Gracie. "An' 'oo are you, then? In't seen yer before."

"Gracie Phipps, ma'am," Gracie replied.

"Never 'eard of yer. Still an' all, I 'spec yer'd like a cup o' tea. That daft Jimmy kept yer standin' out there in the cold. Goin' ter snow, like as not, before the day's out."

"They come about Alf," Jimmy explained.

"Course they 'ave." She took the kettle off the hob, warmed an enormous white and wine-colored teapot with half a handle, then made the tea, spooning the leaves from a caddy with an Indian woman painted on the front. "Got no milk," she apologized. "Yer'll 'ave ter 'ave it straight. Give yer 'alf a spoon of 'oney?"

"Thank you," Gracie accepted, and took the same for Minnie Maude.

When they were sitting on a random collection of chairs, Mrs. Quick expressed her approval of Uncle Alf, and her sympathy for Minnie Maude, and then for Bertha. "Too bad for 'er," she said, shaking her head. "That bruvver of 'ers is more trouble than 'e's worth. Pity it weren't 'im as got done in."

"Wouldn't 'ave 'appened to 'im," Jimmy said miserably.

"I reckon as it were that golden tin, or wotever it were," she said, giving Jimmy a sharp look, and shaking her head again. " 'E said as 'e thought they never meant ter put it out."

Minnie Maude sat up sharply, nearly spilling her tea. "Wot were that, then?" she asked eagerly.

Jimmy glanced at his wife. "Don't go puttin' ideas inter 'er 'ead. We never saw no gold tin. It were jus' Tommy Cob ramblin' on." He turned to Minnie Maude. "It ain't nothin'. Folk put out all kinds o' things. Never know why, an' it don't do ter ask."

"A golden box?" Minnie Maude said in amazement. " 'Oo'd put out summink like that?"

"Nobody," Jimmy agreed. "It were jus' Tommy talkin' like a fool. Prob'ly an old piece o' brass, like as not, or even painted wood, or summink."

"Mebbe that's why they killed Uncle Alf an' took the cart?" Minnie Maude was sitting clutching her porcelain teacup, her eyes wide with fear. "An' Charlie."

"Don' be daft!" Jimmy said wearily. "If they put out summink by mistake, then they'd jus' go an' ask fer it back. Mebbe give 'im a couple o' bob fer it, not go off killin' people."

"But they did kill 'im," Minnie Maude pointed out, sniffing and letting out her breath in a long sigh. " 'E's dead."

"I know," Jimmy admitted. "An' I'm real sorry about that. 'Ave some more 'ot water in yer tea?"

That was all they would learn from him, and ten minutes later they were outside in the street again, and a fine rain was falling with a drift of sleet now and then.

"I've still gotta find Charlie," Minnie Maude said, staring ahead of her, avoiding Gracie's eyes. "Uncle Alf doin' Jimmy's round jus' makes it worse. Charlie's really lorst now!"

"I know that," Gracie agreed.

Minnie Maude stopped abruptly on the cobbles. "Yer think as there's summink real bad 'appened, don't yer!" It was a challenge, not a question.

Gracie took a deep breath. "I dunno wot I think," she admitted. She was about to add that she thought Jimmy Quick was not telling all the truth, then she decided not to. It would only upset Minnie Maude, and it was just a feeling, nothing as clear as an idea.

"I told yer 'e were a lyin' sod," Minnie Maude said very quietly. "It's written clear as day on 'is face."

"Mebbe 'e's jus' sad cos 'e liked yer uncle Alf," Gracie suggested. "An' if Alf'd bin on 'is own round, mebbe somebody'd 'ave 'elped 'im. But 'e could a still bin dead."

"Yer mean not left lyin' in the roadway." Minnie Maude sniffed hard, but it did not stop the tears from running down her face. "Yer'd 'ave liked Uncle Alf," she said almost accusingly. "'E'd a made yer laugh."

Gracie would have liked to have an uncle who made her laugh. Come to think of it, she'd have liked a donkey who was a friend. They'd known lots of animals in the country, before her mother had died and she'd come to London: sheep, horses, pigs, cows. Not that there was a lot of time for friends now that she was thirteen. Minnie Maude had a lot to learn about reality, which was a shame.

"Yeah," Gracie agreed. "I 'spec I would."

They walked in silence for a while, back toward Brick Lane, and then Thrawl Street. It got colder with every moment.

"Wot are we gonna do?" Minnie Maude asked when they came to the curb and stopped, traffic rattling past them.

Gracie had been thinking. "Go back 'ome an' see if Charlie's come back on 'is own," she replied. " 'E could 'ave."

"D'yer think?" Minnie Maude's voice lifted with hope, and Gracie was touched by a pang of guilt. She had suggested it only because she could think of nothing better.

Gracie did not answer, and they walked the rest of the way past the end of the notorious Flower and Dean Walk in silence, passing figures moving in the shadows. Others stood still, watching and waiting. The ice made the cobbles slippery. The sleet came down a little harder, stinging their faces and rattling against the stone walls to either side of them in the narrow alleys. The gutters were filling up, water flecked with white that disappeared almost instantly, not yet cold enough to freeze solid. Their breath made white trails of vapor in the air.

Minnie Maude led the way into the back gate of a house exactly like its neighbors on either side. The only thing that distinguished it was the shed at the back, which, from Minnie Maude's sniff and her eager expression, was clearly Charlie's stable. Now she went straight to the door and pushed it open, drawing in her breath to speak, then stood frozen, her shoulders slumping with despair.

Gracie's heart sank, too, although she should have understood better than to imagine the donkey would have come home. She already knew that something was wrong. Probably it was only some minor dishonesty, someone taking advantage of a man who had died suddenly and unexpectedly; a theft, not anything as far-fetched as a murder. But either way, Minnie Maude would hurt just as badly. She would miss the uncle who had made her laugh and had loved her, and the donkey who'd been her friend.

"We'll find 'im," Gracie said impulsively, swallowing hard, and knowing she was making a promise she would not be able to keep.

Minnie Maude forced herself not to cry. She took an enormous breath and turned to face Gracie, her cheeks tear-streaked, wet hair sticking to her forehead. "Yeah. Course we will," she agreed. She led the way along the rest of the short path, barely glancing up as a couple of pigeons flapped above her and disappeared into the loft over the stable. She pushed the back door of the house open, and Gracie followed her inside.

A thin woman with a plain face stood over a chopping board slicing carrots and turnips, her

large-knuckled hands red from the cold. She had
the most beautiful hair Gracie had ever seen. In
the lantern light it was burnished like autumn
leaves, a warm color, as if remembering the sun.
She looked up as Minnie Maude came in, then her
pale eyes widened a little as she saw Gracie, and
her hands stopped working.

"W'ere yer bin, Minnie Maude?"

"Lookin' for Charlie," Minnie Maude replied.
"This is Gracie, from 'Eneage Street. She's 'elpin'
me."

Aunt Bertha shook her head. "In't no point,"
she said quietly. " 'E'll come 'ome by 'isself . . . or 'e
won't. In't nothing yer can do, child. An' don't go
wastin' other folks' time." She regarded Gracie
with only the tiniest fraction of curiosity. There
were dozens of children up and down every street,
and there was nothing remarkable about her.
"Good o' yer, but in't nothin' yer can do. 'E must a
got a scare when poor Alf died." She started chopping the turnip again.

" 'E wouldn't be able ter find 'isself," Minnie Maude agreed. " 'E weren't on 'is own route. 'E were on Jimmy Quick's."

"Don't talk nonsense, Minnie," Bertha said briskly. "Course 'e weren't. Why'd 'e be down there?" She chopped harder, drawing the knife through the tough vegetables with renewed force. "Yer got chores ter get on with." She looked at Gracie. "Yer got 'em too, I 'spec."

It was on the edge of Gracie's tongue to say to Bertha that she'd sold Charlie, and why couldn't she just be honest enough to tell Minnie Maude so. Then at least she wouldn't be worrying about him being lost and hungry, wandering around in the sleet, wet and maybe frightened.

The outside door opened again, and Stan appeared. He looked at Minnie Maude, then at Gracie. "Wot yer doin' back 'ere again?" he said sharply.

"She's 'elpin' me look fer Charlie," Minnie Maude told him.

"She's jus' goin'," Bertha interrupted soothingly. Her face was pinched, her eyes steady on Stan. "She were only 'elpin'."

"Well, yer shouldn't bother folks," Stan told Minnie Maude. "Yer looked. 'E ain't around. Now do like yer told."

" 'E's lorst," Minnie Maude persisted.

"Donkeys don't get lorst," Stan said, and shook his head. " 'E's bin doin' these streets fer years. 'E'll come 'ome, or mebbe somebody took 'im. Which is stealin', an' if I find the bastard, I'll make 'im pay. But that's my business. It in't yers. Now go and do yer chores, girl." He looked at Gracie. "An' you do yers, an' all. Yer must 'ave summink ter do better 'n wanderin' round the streets lookin' fer some damn donkey!"

"But 'e's lorst!" Minnie Maude protested again, standing her ground even though she must have been able to see as well as Gracie could that Stan was angry. " 'E weren't wi' Uncle Alf's—"

"Don't talk nonsense!" Bertha snapped at her,

putting the knife down and raising her hand as if she would slap Minnie Maude around the ears if she did not keep quiet. But it was not anger Gracie could see in her eyes. Gracie was suddenly, in that instant, quite sure that it was fear. She lifted her foot and gave Minnie Maude a sharp kick on the ankle.

Minnie Maude gasped and turned sharply.

"I'm lost an' all," Gracie said. "An' yer aunt Bertha's right, I got chores, too. Can yer show me which way I gotta go? If yer please?"

Shoulders slumped again, wiping her face with her sleeve to hide the tears, Minnie Maude led the way out the back door, past Charlie's empty stable, and into the street.

"Yer right," Gracie said when they were beyond where Bertha or Stan could hear them. "There's summink wrong, but yer uncle Stan don't like yer pokin' inter it, an' I think yer aunt Bertha's scared o' summink."

"She's scared of 'im," Minnie Maude said with

45

a shrug. " 'E's got a nasty temper, an' Alf in't 'ere no more ter keep 'im in 'and, like. Wot are we gonna do?"

"Yer gonna do yer chores, like I am," Gracie replied firmly.

Minnie Maude's mouth pulled tight to stop her lips from trembling. She searched Gracie's face, hope fading in her. She took a shaky breath.

"I gotta think!" Gracie said desperately. "I . . . I in't givin' up." She felt hot and cold at once with the rashness of what she had just said. Instantly she wished to take it back, and it was too late. "In't no sense till we think," she said again.

"Yeah," Minnie Maude agreed. She forced a rather wobbly smile. "I'll go do me chores." And she turned and walked away, heading into the rain.

Gracie went to help Mr. Wiggins, as she did every other day, running errands and cleaning out the one room in which he lived, scrubbing, doing laundry, and making sure he had groceries. He paid her sixpence at the end of each week, which was today. Sometimes he even made it ninepence, if he was feeling really generous.

"Wot's the matter wif yer, then?" he asked as she came into the room from outside, closing the rickety door behind her. She went straight to the corner where the broom and the scrubbing brush and pail were kept. "Got a face on yer like a burst boot, girl," he went on. "In't like you."

"Sorry, Mr. Wiggins. I got a friend in trouble." She glanced at him briefly with something like a smile, then picked up the broom and started to sweep. Her hands were so cold she could hardly hold the wooden shaft firmly enough.

" 'Ave a cup o' tea," he suggested.

"I in't got time. I gotta clean this up."

"Yer 'ere ter please me or yerself, girl?"

She stared at him. "I'm 'ere ter clean the floor an' fetch yer tea an' bread an' taters."

"Ye're 'ere ter do as I tell yer," he contradicted.

"Yer want the floor cleaned or not?"

"I wan' a cup o' tea. Can you tell me why yer look like yer lost sixpence an' found nothin'? Put the kettle on like I said."

She hesitated.

" 'Nother threepence?" he offered.

She couldn't help smiling at him. He was old and crotchety sometimes, but she knew that most of that came from being lonely, and not wanting anyone to know that it hurt him.

"I don' need threepence," she lied. "I'll get a cup o' tea. I'm fair froze any'ow." Obediently she went to the small fire he kept going in a black potbellied stove, and pulled the kettle over. "Yer got any milk, then?" she asked.

"Course I 'ave," he said indignantly. "Usual place. Wot's the matter wif yer, Gracie?"

She made the tea, wondering whether it would be worse to use up what she knew was the last of his milk, and leave him without any, or not to use it, and insult his hospitality. She knew with her gran the humiliation would have stung more, so she used it.

" 'S good," she said, sitting opposite him and sipping it gingerly.

"So wot's goin' on, then?" he asked.

She told him about Alf dying and falling off the cart, and Charlie getting lost, and how she didn't know what to do to help Minnie Maude.

He thought in silence for several minutes while they both finished their tea. "I dunno neither," he said at last.

"Well, fanks fer the tea," she said, conquering a very foolish sense of disappointment. What had she expected, anyway? She stood up ready to go back to the sweeping and scrubbing.

"But yer could go and ask Mr. Balthasar." He put his mug down on the scarred tabletop. " 'E's about the cleverest feller I ever 'eard of." He tapped his head with one arthritic finger. "Wise, 'e is. Knows all kinds o' things. Mebbe 'e di'n't know if Alf fell off the cart afore 'e were dead, or after, but if anyone can find a donkey wot's lost—or stole—it'd be 'im."

"Would 'e?" Gracie said with sudden hope.

Mr. Wiggins nodded, smiling.

She had a moment's deep doubt. Mr. Wiggins was old and a bit daft. Maybe he just wanted to help, which didn't mean he could. Still, she had no better idea herself. "I'll go an' see 'im," she promised. "Where is 'e?"

She found the shop of Mr. Balthasar on Whitechapel Road just about where Mr. Wiggins had said it would be, which surprised her. He had seemed to be too vague for her to trust his judgment. But the moment she stepped inside the dark, narrow doorway, she thought it was much less good an idea than Mr. Wiggins had implied. There was no one to be seen in the extraordinary interior, but objects of one sort or another seemed to fill every shelf from floor to ceiling, and be suspended by ropes, threads, and chains from above so that she was afraid to move in case she dislodged something and brought it all crashing down on herself.

There seemed to be an inordinate number of shoes, or perhaps they would more properly be called slippers. She couldn't imagine anyone going outside in the wet street in such things. They were made of cloth, of soft leather, even of velvet, and they were stitched with all sorts of patterns like nothing she had ever seen before. Some had silly curling toes that would make anybody fall over in two steps. But they were beautiful!

There were brass dishes with curly writing all over them, no pictures at all, but the writing was so fancy it would do just as well. And everywhere she looked there were boxes of every kind and shape, painted, decorated with stones, shiny and dull, written on and plain. Some were so small they would have had trouble holding a thimble, others big enough to take your whole hand. And there was an enormous machine that looked like a cross between a boiler and a pipe to smoke, like gentlemen used. Though what use such a contraption might be, she had no idea.

She was still staring when a voice spoke from behind her.

"And what may I do for you, young lady?"

She was so startled she was sure her feet actually came off the floor. She jerked around and looked at the man not three feet away. He had come in silently, and she had heard nothing. He must have been wearing those velvet slippers.

"I . . . ," she began. "I . . ."

He waited. He was tall and lean and his hair was very black, with just a few streaks of white in it at the sides. His skin was coppery dark, his nose high-bridged and aquiline.

She drew in a deep breath. "I need 'elp," she

admitted. This was not a man you lied to. "An' Mr. Wiggins says as ye're the wisest man around 'ere, so I come ter ask."

"Does he indeed?" Mr. Balthasar smiled with a definite trace of amusement. "You have the advantage of me."

"Wot?" She blinked.

"You seem to know something of me," he explained. "I know nothing of you."

"Oh. I'm Gracie Phipps. I live in 'Eneage Street. But I come cos o' Minnie Maude. 'Er uncle Alf got killed, an' Charlie's lost an' could be all on 'is own, an' in trouble."

"I think you had better tell me from the beginning," Mr. Balthasar said gently. "This sounds as if it might be quite a complicated matter, Gracie Phipps."

Gracie drew in her breath and began.

Mr. Balthasar listened without interrupting, nodding now and then.

" . . . so I think as Jimmy Quick in't tellin' the

truth," she said finally. "Cos it don't make no sense. But I still gotta find Charlie, or that daft little article in't gonna give up till summink real bad 'appens."

"No," Mr. Balthasar agreed, and his face was very grim. "I can see that she isn't. But I fear that you are right. Several people may not be telling the truth. And perhaps Minnie Maude is not quite as daft as you imagine."

Gracie gulped. The room with its crowded shelves and endless assortment of treasures seemed smaller than before, closer to her, the walls crowding in. It was oddly silent, as if the street outside were miles away.

"Course she's daft," Gracie said firmly. " 'Oo's gonna kill a rag an' bone man? On purpose, like? 'E jus' died an' fell off, an' as 'e were on Jimmy Quick's patch, 'stead of 'is own, no one knew 'im, so 'e jus' laid there till someone found 'im."

"And what happened to Charlie?" Mr. Balthasar asked very gently.

"Charlie couldn't pick 'im up," Gracie replied. "An' 'e couldn't get 'elp, so 'e jus' stayed there with 'im . . . sort o' . . . waitin'."

"And why was he not there when poor Alf was found?"

Gracie realized her mistake. "I dunno. Someone must a stole 'im."

"And the cart? They stole that also?"

"Must 'ave."

"Yes," Mr. Balthasar said very sincerely. "That, I fear, may be far more serious than you realize." He searched her face, as if trying to judge how much she understood, and how much more he should tell her.

Suddenly she was brushed with genuine fear, a cold grip inside her that held hard. She fought against it. Now it was not just helping Minnie Maude because she was sorry for her, and felt a certain kind of responsibility. She was caught in it herself. She looked back at the strange features, the dark, burning eyes of Mr. Balthasar.

"Why'd anyone steal it?" she said in little more than a whisper.

"Ah." He let out his breath slowly. "There I think you have it, Gracie. What was in it that someone believed to be worth a human life in order to steal?"

Gracie shivered. "I dunno." The words barely escaped her lips. "D'yer think 'e really were killed?" It still seemed ridiculous, something Minnie Maude would make up, because she was only eight, and daft as a brush. Gracie swallowed hard. It was no longer a bit of a nuisance. She was scared. "She jus' wants 'er friend Charlie back, an' safe."

Mr. Balthasar did not answer her.

"D'yer think they done 'im in, too?" Her voice wobbled a bit, and she could not help it.

"I doubt it," he replied, but there was not even the ghost of a smile on his copper-colored face. "But be very careful, Gracie. It sounds to me as if it is possible that Minnie Maude's uncle saw something he was not supposed to, or picked up something that was intended for someone else. You are quite sure you have the details correct?"

She nodded, her eyes not leaving his steady gaze. "'E done Jimmy Quick's round fer 'im, an' about 'alfway, or more, 'e died, an' Charlie an' the cart, an' everythin' in it, were gone."

"And which streets were Jimmy Quick's round?"

"I dunno."

"But you said you and Minnie Maude went there, at least some of the way."

Gracie looked down at her boots. "We did. I know where I went left, an' where I went right, but I can't read the names."

"I see. Of course." There was apology in his voice, as if he should have known she couldn't read.

"I could find 'em again . . . I think," she offered, her cheeks hot with shame.

"No doubt." He smiled now, very briefly, then

the gravity returned. "But I think it would be wiser if you didn't. Donkeys are patient and useful beasts. Only a fool would hurt them. Charlie will be miserable for a little while, but he will be all right."

He was lying to her, and she knew it. She had seen donkeys starved, beaten, shaking with cold and fear.

He saw it in her face, and now it was his turn to be ashamed. "I'm sorry," he said humbly. "You are right to fear. I will see if I can learn anything. But in the meantime, you should say nothing, and ask no further questions. Do you understand?"

"Yeah."

He did not look satisfied. "Are you sure?"

She nodded.

"What do you know about Uncle Alf?" he persisted.

"'E were funny an' kind, an' 'e made Minnie Maude laugh, and she said 'e knew about all sorts o' places, and things. 'E saw things in like . . .

58

brighter colors than wot most people do." She took a deep breath, overcome with her own sense of the loss of something she had only imagined—a companion who'd had dreams and ideas, whose mind had been far away from disappointment and tired streets. She wondered what Uncle Alf had looked like. She saw him with white hair, a bit wild, as if he had been out in a great wind. He would have blue eyes that saw either very close or very far indeed, all the way to the horizon.

Then a flash of memory came to her of what Dora Quick had said, and Jimmy had been angry about.

Balthasar must have seen it in her face. "What is it, Gracie?"

"Mrs. Quick said as Alf picked up a gold-colored box that were special, real beautiful."

"How did she know that?" he said quickly.

"It were someone called Cob wot told 'er. But Mr. Quick said 'e were talkin' daft, an' ter take no notice. An' she never said any more."

"I see. I think that is extremely good advice, Gracie. Say nothing more either. Above all, do not mention the casket."

"Wot's a casket?" she asked.

"A special kind of box to keep precious things in. Now go home and do your chores. I shall look into the matter."

She blinked, staring back at him. " 'Ow'll I know if yer do?"

"Because I shall send a message to you in Heneage Street."

"Oh. Thank you . . . Mr. . . . . Balthasar."

*G*racie completed her work as soon as possible, knowing she was skimping, and telling herself she would make a better job of it tomorrow. As soon as the cleaning looked finished, at the quickest glance, no rubbing fingers over things to make sure, she wrapped herself up in her heavy brown wool shawl. Tying it tight under her chin so it was thick and lumpy to keep the rain out, she raced into the street holding her head down against the wind and the sleet. She knew the way to Minnie Maude's house even without having to look, never mind ask, and she was there inside ten minutes.

She stopped well short of the house itself. She was a little bit in awe of Aunt Bertha, and she definitely did not want to encounter Stan again. Although since he was a hansom cabbie and it was a bitter day just short of Christmas, there should have been any amount of trade for him in the streets a little farther west, so he was unlikely to be home.

Still she waited, shivering in a doorway opposite, holding her shawl tighter and tighter around her, in spite of the fact that it was wet most of the way through. Eventually she saw Minnie Maude opening the door. She stepped out, her pale, little face bleak, looking one way and then another as if perhaps Charlie might come down the cobbles, in spite of all reason.

"Stupid little article!" Gracie said savagely to herself. " 'E in't comin' 'ome!" She found her own voice choking, and was angry. It wasn't her donkey! She'd never even seen him.

She moved out of the doorway and marched across the uneven road, her boots sloshing in the puddles where stones were missing and the water had collected.

Minnie Maude saw her immediately, and her face brightened into a wide smile.

Gracie's heart sank. She could do nothing to justify it. She waited while Minnie Maude went back inside and then barely a moment later opened the door again and came clattering across the road.

"Yer find out summink?" she said eagerly, her eyes bright.

Gracie hated it. "Nuffink for certain sure," she

replied. "But I told a wise man about it, an' 'e thinks as there could be summink bad. 'E said ter leave it alone."

Minnie Maude's eyes never left Gracie's. "But we in't goin' ter . . ."

Gracie shivered. The wind was cutting down the street like a knife.

"Come up inter the stable," Minnie Maude said quickly. "It's warm in there, up where the pigeons are. Anyway, I gotta feed them, since Uncle Alf in't 'ere anymore." There was only a slight quiver in her voice, and she turned away from Gracie to hide the look on her face. Because she concealed it, it was even more telling.

Gracie followed her back across the street, tugging at her shawl to keep it around her shoulders. They went around and in through the back gate, then across the cobbles to the stable door. This was where Charlie had lived, and Gracie stared at the rough brick walls and the straw piled on the floor. She noticed that Minnie Maude walked through so quickly that she could hardly have seen anything but a blur of familiar shapes.

In the next tiny room, half-filled with hay, a rough ladder was propped up against the edge of the loft, and Minnie Maude hitched up her skirts and scrambled up it. "C'mon," she invited encouragingly. "I'll 'old the top fer yer." And as soon as she reached the ledge of the upper floor, she rolled over sideways and then knelt, gripping the two uprights of the ladder and hanging on to them. She peered down at Gracie, waiting for her.

Wondering where her wits had gone to, Gracie grasped her skirts halfway up her legs and climbed up, hanging on desperately with her other hand. She reached the top white-knuckled and cursing under her breath. Some days she doubted she still had the sense she was born with.

"Careful!" Minnie Maude warned a trifle sharply as Gracie swayed. "Yer don' wanna tip it off. We'd 'ave ter jump, and there in't nuffink ter land on."

Gracie clung on desperately, feeling her head whirl and her stomach knot. She said nothing, concentrating fiercely on what she was doing. She couldn't let Minnie Maude see how scared she was. Minnie Maude would lose all trust in her. She took a deep breath and drew herself up onto the ledge, teetering for a moment, her legs in the air, then scrambled forward and fell flat on her face. She sat up, trying to look as if nothing at all had happened.

" 'Is name was Mr. Balthasar," she said solemnly.

There was a kind of whir of wings and a clatter as a pigeon burst through the narrow entrance in the roof and landed on the wood. Minnie Maude ignored it. Gracie felt her heart nearly burst out of her chest.

"Did 'e say as summink 'ad 'appened ter Uncle Alf?" Minnie Maude asked.

" 'E di'n't rightly know," Gracie said honestly. "But 'e reckoned as it were bad, cos o' them takin' the cart, an' all." She lowered her voice. "Minnie

65

Maude, 'e said as 'e thought the golden box were a casket, an' could be summink really important, an' mebbe that's why Uncle Alf were killed. 'E said as we shouldn't go on lookin' fer it, in case we get 'urt as well."

"But wot about Charlie?" Minnie Maude asked.

"'E said as donkeys are useful, so they'll prob'ly look after 'im, feed 'im, an' give 'im somewhere ter stay." She remembered Mr. Balthasar's face as he had said it, the dark, sad look in his eyes. She had seen that look before. He did not mean it. He had said it to comfort her. Now she was saying it again, to comfort Minnie Maude.

Minnie Maude stared in front of her. "'S all right," she said quietly. "Yer don't 'ave ter look fer Charlie. I un'erstand."

"I di'n't say I weren't gonna look fer 'im!" Gracie retorted with indignation. "I'm jus' tellin' yer wot 'e said!"

Minnie Maude raised her eyes very slowly, bright with hope.

Gracie could have kicked herself, but there was no escape. "We gotta think fast," she warned.

"It's cold," Minnie Maude replied, as if it were the natural thing to say. "Let's go over inter the 'ay." And without waiting for agreement, she tucked her skirt up again and crawled back into the dark, rich-smelling crowded space in the corner. She went into it headfirst, then swiveled around, and a moment later her face appeared and she smiled encouragingly, a long wisp of hay behind her ear.

Gracie had no dignified choice but to follow her. She tucked her skirts up also and crawled across the space to the bales, then pushed her way in, twisted around, and sat down. It was prickly, but it smelled nice, and it brought back dim memories of the past, of being in the country, long ago. She imagined in time it would be quite warm where they were, compared with the stone floor below.

"Summink really important," Minnie Maude said thoughtfully. "S'pose it would 'ave ter be, ter put it in a casket, an' all." She sat motionless, her eyes very wide. "D'yer think it's magic?"

"What?"

"Magic," Minnie Maude repeated, her voice hushed with awe.

"Wotever put that inter yer 'ead, yer daft little article?" Gracie demanded. "In't no such thing." Then the minute she had said it, she wished she hadn't. Minnie Maude was only eight. Gracie should have let her have a year or two more of dreams.

"There's Christmas," Minnie Maude whispered, her eyes brimming with tears.

Gracie struggled desperately to retrieve the loss. "That in't magic," she answered. "That's . . . that's God. It's diff'rent."

Minnie Maude blushed. "Is it?"

"Course it is." Gracie's mind was whirling like the wind.

Minnie Maude waited, staring at her.

"Magic don't 'ave rules," Gracie explained. "An'

bad people can do it as well as good. It in't always nice. Wot God does is always nice, even if it don't look much like it at the time."

" 'Ow d'yer know?" Minnie Maude asked reasonably.

Gracie was not going to be careful this time. "I dunno," she admitted. "I jus' know."

"Is it an 'oly casket?" Minnie Maude asked her.

"Wot would an 'oly casket be doin' out in the street fer a rag an' bone man ter pick up?" Gracie tried to put the conversation back into some kind of reality.

"Jesus were born in a stable," Minnie Maude pointed out. "Like wot we're in."

"This is a dovecote," Gracie replied.

"It's a stable downstairs, cos Charlie lived in it." Minnie Maude sniffed.

Gracie felt an overwhelming helplessness. She longed to be able to comfort Minnie Maude, but did not know how to. "Yer right," she agreed, avoiding Minnie Maude's eyes. "I forgot that."

"Mebbe it's a present?" Minnie Maude went on. "Mr. Balthasar's a wise man. Yer said so. It could a got stole, an' that's why 'e knows about it. 'E said it were bad, I mean real bad. Ter steal from God, in't that about as bad as yer can be?"

Her logic was faultless. Gracie felt a chill run through her, as if some inner part of her had been touched by ice. She hugged her arms closer around her, and the pigeons cooing seemed louder, as though the birds too were afraid.

"We gotta get it back," Minnie Maude said, moving a little closer to Gracie. "Mebbe Christmas won't 'appen if we don't—"

"Course it'll 'appen!" Gracie said instantly, her voice sharp, too positive.

"Will it?" Minnie Maude whispered. "Yer sure? Even if it were stole by someone wicked? I mean not just bad, but terrible . . . like . . . the devil?"

Gracie had no opinion on that. It was something she had not even thought of. It was a child's imagination, and she was old enough to face the real problems in the world, like cold and hunger, illness, and how to pay for things. She had grown out of fairies and goblins a long time ago, about the time when she'd left the country and had come to live in London. But Minnie Maude was years younger, a child still. Her neck was so pale and slender it was surprising it could hold her head up, and not all her teeth were fully grown in. She believed in magic, good and bad, and in miracles. It would be like breaking a dream to tell her differently.

"Yeah," Gracie answered, her fingers crossed under the hay, where Minnie Maude couldn't see them. "But if 'ooever took it is real bad, then we gotta be careful. We gotta think 'ard before we do anyfink daft."

"If they're real bad, they might 'urt Charlie," Minnie Maude said with a wobble in her voice.

"Wot for? A sick donkey in't no use. Bad in't the same as stupid." Gracie said it with far more conviction than she felt. She had to add something else quickly, before Minnie Maude had time to argue. "If Uncle Alf took the box wot's a casket, Mr. Balthasar said, then wot did 'e do with it?"

"Nuffink," Minnie Maude answered straight-away. "They come after 'im an' took it."

"Then why'd they kill 'im?" Gracie said reason-ably. "An' why take Charlie and the cart? That's stupid. Then they got a dead body, an' a donkey an' a cart wot's stole. Fer what?" She shook her head with increasing conviction. "They di'n't find the gold box, or they'd a left the cart. They took Char-lie cos they 'ad ter take the cart an' they couldn't pull it without 'im."

"Why'd they kill Uncle Alf? 'E should a jus' give it back ter 'em."

"I dunno. Mebbe they di'n't mean ter," Gracie suggested. "Mebbe 'e argued wif 'em, cos 'e wanted ter keep it."

Minnie Maude shook her head. " 'E weren't like that. Less, o' course, 'e knew as they were wicked?" Minnie Maude blinked. "D'yer reckon as 'e knew? 'E were wise. 'E knew when people told the truth an' when they was lyin', even strangers. An' 'e could tell the time, an' wot the weather were gonna do."

Gracie had no idea. She tried to visualize Uncle Alf from what Minnie Maude had told her, and all she could see was a man with white hair and blue eyes who liked to make children laugh, who did a favor for Jimmy Quick, and who kept his donkey in a warm stable that smelled of hay—and pigeons. What kind of person understood evil? Good people? Wise people? People who had faced it and come out hurt but had ultimately survived?

"Mebbe," she said at length. "If 'e 'ad it, an' 'e knew wot it were, then wot'd 'e do wif it?"

Minnie Maude thought about it for so long that Gracie had just about decided she was not going to answer, when finally she did. " 'E 'ad a special place where 'e put secret things. We could look there. If 'e got 'ome wif it, 'e'd a put it there."

Gracie thought it unlikely that poor Alf had

ever reached his home, but it would be silly not to at least try. There might be something else that would give them a clue.

Minnie Maude stood up and went back to the ladder.

Gracie's stomach clenched at the thought of going down it again. It would be even worse than going up. She watched Minnie Maude's hands on the uprights. She was holding on, but her knuckles were not white. She moved as easily as if it were a perfectly ordinary staircase. Gracie would have to do the same. If Minnie Maude knew she was afraid, how could the little girl have any confidence in her? How could she feel any better, and believe Gracie could fight real evil, if she couldn't even go backward down a rickety ladder?

"Are yer comin'?" Minnie Maude called from the stable floor.

There was a flurry of wings, and another pigeon landed and strutted across the floor, looking at Gracie curiously.

"Yeah," Gracie answered, and gritted her teeth. Tucking her skirt up, she went down the steps with barely a hesitation.

"This way," Minnie Maude said, and started across the floor, kicking the straw out of the way with her scuffed boots. There was a half archway leading into another room where bales of straw were stacked on one side, and harnesses hung on hooks on the wall on the other side.

"They're extra," Minnie Maude said, swallowing back a sudden rush of tears. "Yer always need extra pieces, in case summink gets broke. Charlie'll 'ave the real harness on 'im."

Gracie looked at the worn leather, the old brasses polished thin, the rings, buckles, and bits, and felt the overwhelming loss wash over her. These were like the clothes of a person who was missing, maybe even hurt or dead. She stared at the objects, trying to think of something to say, and she noticed the scars on the whitewash of the wall. It looked as if somebody had banged against it, and then drawn something sharp for a couple of inches, digging into the stone. The white of the lime covering it was cut through and flaking.

She turned slowly. Minnie Maude was staring at it too.

Gracie's eyes went to the floor. It was flat cement, uneven, half-covered now with loose pieces of hay from the bales. There were more scuff marks, scratches, and brown stains, as if something wet had been spilled, and then stood in. Whatever it was had been smeared. Perhaps someone had slipped.

"Gracie . . . ," Minnie Maude whispered, putting out her hand. "Summink bad 'appened 'ere."

She was cold when Gracie touched her. Gracie meant to hold Minnie Maude's hand gently, but found she was gripping, squashing Minnie Maude's thin little fingers. It did not even occur to her to lie. This was not the time or the place for it.

"I know." She thought of telling her that it

might not have been Charlie's blood, but it didn't need saying. Somebody had been hurt here.

"Gold's precious," Minnie Maude went on. "Lot o' money. But it must a bin more 'n that, eh?"

"Yeah," Gracie agreed. "Summink inside it."

"A present for God?"

"Mebbe."

"Wot d'yer give God, then? In't 'e already got everyfink'?" Minnie Maude asked.

Gracie shook her head. "I dunno. Mebbe it in't fer 'im."

Minnie Maude's eyes widened. "I never thought o' that. Wot d'yer think it could be?"

"It must be summink very precious," Gracie replied. "And I think we gotta find it."

"Yeah." Minnie Maude nodded vigorously. "We 'ave."

Minnie Maude turned toward the door just as it flew open and Stan strode in, broad, bowlegged, his face twisted with anger.

"Wot yer doin' in 'ere, missie?" he demanded of Minnie Maude. Then, swinging around to Gracie, he said, "An' you don't belong 'ere neither! Leave! Out of 'ere!" He waved his arms as though to force them out.

Minnie Maude stood as if frozen.

"Go on!" Stan shouted. "In't yer got no chores ter do, yer lazy little girl? Think yer 'ere fer us ter feed yer gob while yer sit 'ere in the 'ay day-dreamin'?"

Minnie Maude started to say something, then saw his hand swinging wide to clip her round the side of the head, and ducked out of his way. She turned to stare at Gracie. "C'mon!" she warned, making for the door, and escape.

Gracie wanted to stay and argue, but she knew better. There was an anger in Stan's face that was deeper than mere temper. There was a shadow of fear in it also, and she knew that people who were frightened were dangerous. Something very bad indeed had happened in this place, and the taste of it put wings on her feet. She veered sideways and shot past his outstretched hand, through the open door, and down the path to the alleyway.

Through the back gate she nearly bumped into Minnie Maude.

"Yer all right?" Minnie Maude asked anxiously.

"Yeah." Gracie pushed her hair back and straightened her rumpled skirt, then picked a few pieces of hay from her shawl.

"Wot are we gonna do?" Minnie Maude asked.

Gracie felt as if she were jumping into a fast, icy river. The only thing worse would be being left on the bank.

"We're gonna find out exactly where Uncle Alf went the day 'e were killed," she answered, as if that had been her decision all along.

" 'Ow are we gonna do that?"

"We're gonna ask Jimmy Quick wot way 'e went, an' then foller it an' find out 'oo saw Uncle Alf the same way. They might know, cos of it bein' someone diff'rent than Jimmy."

"Then wot?" Minnie Maude's eyes did not flicker an instant.

Gracie's mind raced. "Then we'll find out where 'e were killed, exact like, an' 'oo 'e saw, an' 'oo 'e di'n't."

Minnie Maude gulped. "Then we'll know 'oo killed 'im?"

The thought was enormous, and terrifying. Suddenly it did not seem so clever at all. In fact it seemed the depth of stupidity. "No we won't," Gracie said sharply. "We'll just know where 'e might a picked up the casket . . . an' o' course where 'e couldn't've, since 'e in't bin there yet."

Minnie Maude looked hopeful. "We'll go and see Jimmy Quick." She squinted up at the sky. "We could get there now, but 'e won't be 'ome yet."

Gracie was more concerned with thinking of a good reason to go back to ask Jimmy Quick about the route he took, so they could explain why they asked.

"Wot's the matter?" Minnie Maude demanded, the fear back in her voice.

"Nuffink," Gracie said immediately, wondering why she was suddenly putting off telling the truth. "Jus' planning wot ter say, cos why we want ter know? Jimmy Quick in't silly. 'E's gonna ask. We gotta 'ave summink ter say as could be true."

"We wanna know w'ere me Uncle Alf died," Minnie Maude said, watching Gracie carefully. "I'm gonna put a flower there."

" 'Ave yer got one?" Gracie said reasonably. "I got twopence. We could buy some . . . if yer like?"

Minnie Maude nodded. "Thank yer. That's . . ." She searched for a word for the complicated emotion. "Good," she finished, unsatisfied.

Gracie smiled at her, and suddenly Minnie Maude beamed back, her whole face lit with gratitude. They had a plan.

"We'll go ter see Jimmy Quick this evening," Gracie said decisively. "If we wait till termorrer, 'e'll mebbe take us, an' we don't want 'im ter, cos we need ter ask questions it's better as 'e don't know."

Minnie Maude nodded vigorously.

"I'll meet yer 'ere, at 'alf past lights on," Gracie went on. She looked up at the lamppost just above where they stood. "Watch for the lamplighter. 'E's usually reg'lar. Yer wait, if I in't 'ere right away."

Minnie Maude nodded again.

$\mathcal{G}$racie continued with her duties for the day, missing some out and working double speed at others. She tried not to think of the wild promises she had made to Minnie Maude Mudway. She must have lost all the sense she'd ever had! Now she was scrubbing the kitchen bench, lye stinging her hands, fingers wet and cold. The sleet outside was turning to snow, everyone else was thinking of Christmas, and she was planning to go and ask a rag and bone man what his route was, so she could look for the people who had murdered Alf Mudway for a casket! Oh—and the real purpose of the whole thing was to find a donkey, who was probably as right as rain somewhere else, and not sparing them a thought in its head. If donkeys had thoughts.

Then on the other hand, he might be wandering around alone, lost, scared stiff, knowing his master was dead, because he had seen it happen. He could be shivering, wet and frightened, not knowing what to do about it—and hungry. She imagined him, standing in the dark and the rain, ears down, tail down, slowly getting wetter and wetter. She really didn't have any choice.

Added to which, if she didn't help, then Minnie Maude would go off and do it on her own. Gracie knew that without doubt, because Minnie Maude was only eight, and had no idea what she was doing. And Aunt Bertha didn't care. Somebody had to look after Minnie Maude, just like Minnie Maude had to look after Charlie. Some things couldn't be helped, no matter how daft they were, and how much you knew better.

Which is why she kept running out at the back to see if the lamplighter had been yet, and when she saw the light in the distance, she lied to her gran that she had promised old Mrs. Dampier to run an errand for her. Mrs. Dampier never remembered anything, so she wouldn't know. Gracie slipped out of the kitchen into the rain before she could answer the inevitable questions.

Minnie Maude was waiting for her, standing huddled in the shadows, her shawl wrapped around her head and shoulders, skirts flapping damply in the gusty wind, boots soaked. But her face lit with happiness when she saw Gracie, and she darted out of the shelter of the wall and fell in step beside her without giving her time to hesitate or say anything more than " 'Ello."

" 'E'll be 'ome now," Minnie Maude said, skipping a step to match her stride with Gracie's. " 'Avin' 'is tea. We'll ask 'im."

They walked in silence, their feet echoing on the cobbles. The snow had almost stopped, and it was beginning to freeze hard in the few places where it lay. It was wise to watch for icy patches, so as not to slip. Most of the lamps were lit, and there was a yellow warmth to them, like lighted windows to some palace of the mind. There was a slight fog rising, muffling the sound of distant wheels, and every now and then the mournful bellow of a foghorn sounded somewhere down on the river.

There wasn't much to show that Christmas was only a couple of days away, just the occasional wreath of leaves on a door, some with bright berries; or someone passing by singing a snatch of a song, happy and lilting, not the usual bawdy version of the latest from the music halls. In daylight, of course, there might have been a barrel organ, but this was far too late.

They reached Jimmy Quick's gate and made their way across the yard carefully to avoid the clutter, not wanting either to knock anything over or to bash their shins on a crate or old chair.

Jimmy was not pleased to see them. He stood in the doorway, looking immense, with the kitchen candles wavering in the draft behind him and making his shadow loom and bend.

"What d'yer want now, Minnie Maude? Yer gettin' ter be a nuisance," he said angrily. "I can't tell yer nothin', 'ceptin' I'm sorry Alf's dead. I dunno wot 'appened ter 'im. I only know it in't my fault, an' yer can come as many times as yer like, it still in't. I don't owe yer a bleeding thing!"

"Course," Minnie Maude said generously. Standing behind her, Gracie could see that she was shaking, but she kept her eyes on Jimmy's. "I jus' wanted ter ask yer wot way yer goes, so I can find the place 'e died, exact like."

"Wot for?" he said with amazement. " 'E's dead, girl. Goin' starin' at a place in't gonna change nothin'."

Minnie Maude took a deep breath. "I know that. But I wanter put a flower there. 'E should a bin with us for Christmas," she added.

Jimmy Quick swore under his breath. "Yer don't never let go, do yer? I already told yer where 'e were found. Yer got 'oles in yer 'ead, yer don't remember? 'E were in Richard Street, like I said."

Minnie Maude was temporarily speechless.

Jimmy stepped back to close the door.

" 'Ow d'yer get there?" Gracie asked him.

"Yer 'ere an' all?" He peered at her as if, in the shadows, he had not seen her. "Why d'yer care?"

Gracie decided to attack. "Look at 'er!" she told him angrily. "Size of 'er. She'd make a twopenny rabbit look good. Can't go an' leave 'er ter do it on 'er own, can I? She in't got no ma, 'er aunt Bertha don't wanna know—she's got 'er own griefs—an' Stan wouldn't throw a bucket o' water on 'er if she were on fire, let alone take 'er ter Richard Street. Alf were all she 'ad. Wot's the matter wif yer?

Can't yer jus' tell 'er which way ter go?" She scowled as if she found him highly suspicious. "Summink wrong wif it, then?"

"Course there in't, yer daft little girl," he said sharply, then he rattled off a list of streets, and she closed her eyes, concentrating on remembering them, before she looked back at him and thanked him. Then she grabbed Minnie Maude by the hand and retreated into the darkness and the jumble of the yard, pulling Minnie Maude with her. She was not ready to speak yet. She needed to concentrate on memorizing the streets, before they went out of her head. She wished she could write, then they could be kept safe longer. She could bring them back anytime she wanted—days from now, weeks even. One day she would learn, then she'd be able to keep every idea that mattered, forever. That would be like owning the whole world! You could always have people talking to you, telling you their dreams, their ideas. She would do it, absolutely definitely—one day.

She repeated the street names one more time, then turned to Minnie Maude.

"We'll go termorrer," she told her. "You say the streets over an' over, too, case I forget."

"I got 'em." Minnie Maude nodded. "When termorrer?"

Gracie started to walk briskly back toward their own streets, Minnie Maude's first, then hers. They were facing the wind now, and it was colder. "Termorrer," she said.

*I*n the morning, shreds of the fog still lingered. The air was as still as the dead, a rime of ice covered the stones so that they were slick underfoot, and all the gutters were frozen over.

Gracie found Minnie Maude in the usual place, her shawl hugged around her, hands hidden under it. Every few moments the girl banged her feet on the ground to jar them into life. The instant she saw Gracie, she came forward and the two girls fell into step, walking quickly to begin their detection.

Gracie recited the streets over in her mind, trying to make a pattern out of them, so she wouldn't forget.

"I'm gonna learn ter read," she muttered to herself as they trudged along.

"Me, too," Minnie Maude added.

Cannon Street was busy with lots of carts and drays, and a sweeper to keep the manure off the main crossings at the corners. He was working hard now, his arms swinging the broom with considerable force as he got rid of the last droppings left only a few minutes before. It was difficult to tell how old he was. He was less than five feet tall, but his narrow shoulders looked strong. His trousers were too long for him, and frayed at the bottoms over his boots. His coat came past his knees, and his cap rested on his ears. When he smiled at them, they could see that one of his front teeth was broken short, and for a moment his round face gave him the illusion of being about six.

"There y'are!" he said cheerfully, standing back to show the clean path across.

Gracie wished she had a penny to spare him, but he probably had more than she did. But she had a ha'penny, and he might also have information. She gave it to him.

He looked surprised, but he took it. For an instant, she felt rich, and grown-up. "D'yer know Alf, the rag an' bone man wot got killed on Richard Street three days back?" she asked hopefully. " 'E done Jimmy Quick's round."

" 'E 'ad a donkey," Minnie Maude added.

The boy thought for a while, frowning. "Yeah. It'd rained summink 'orrible. Gutters was all swillin' over. 'Ardly worth both'rin'." He jerked the broom at the cobbles to demonstrate.

"Yer saw 'im?" Minnie Maude said excitedly. "Which way were 'e goin'?"

The boy frowned at her, and pointed east into the wind. "That way. Thought as 'e were orff 'is path. Jimmy'd a gorn up there." He swung around and pointed westward, the way they had come. "Still an' all, wot's it matter? Poor devil. S'pose the cold got 'im."

Minnie Maude shook her head. " 'E were done in. Somebody 'it 'im."

"Garn!" the boy said with disbelief. "Why'd anyone do that?"

"Cos 'e knowed summink," Gracie said rapidly. "Mebbe 'e see'd summink as 'e weren't meant ter."

The boy's eyes widened. "Then yer shouldn't go lookin', or mebbe yer'll know it, too! In't yer got no more sense?"

" 'E weren't yer uncle," Gracie responded, liking the sound of it, as if Alf had been hers. It gave her a kind of warmth inside. Then she thought of drawing the sweeper into it a bit more personally. "Wot's yer name?"

"Monday," he replied.

"Monday?" Minnie Maude said, and stared at him.

His face tightened a bit, as if the wind were colder. "I started on a Monday," he explained.

She shrugged. "I dunno when I started. Mebbe I in't really started yet?"

"Yeah yer 'ave," Gracie said quickly. "Yer gonna find Charlie. That's a good way ter start." She turned back to Monday. "When were Alf 'ere, an' where'd 'e go? We gotta find out. An' tell us again, but do it clear, cos we don' know this patch. It was Jimmy Quick's, not Uncle Alf's."

Monday screwed up his face. " 'E went that way, which weren't the way Jimmy Quick goes. I see'd 'im go right down there, then 'e turned the corner, that way." He jerked his hand leftward. "An' I dunno where 'e went after that."

"That's the wrong way," Minnie Maude said, puzzled. "I remembered it." She recited the streets as Jimmy Quick had told them, ticking them off on her fingers.

"Well that's the way 'e went." Monday was firm.

They thanked him and set off in the direction he had pointed.

"Were 'e lorst?" Minnie Maude said when they were on the far side and well out of the traffic.

"I dunno," Gracie admitted. Her mind was racing, imagining all kinds of things. This was later in the route. He couldn't have done all the little alleys to the west so soon. Why had he been going the wrong way? Had somebody been after him already? No, that didn't make any sense.

"We gotta find somebody else ter ask," she said aloud. " 'Oo else would a seen 'im?"

Minnie Maude thought about it for some time before she answered. They walked another hundred yards along Cannon Street, but no one could help.

"Nobody seen 'im," Minnie Maude said, fighting tears. "We in't never gonna find Charlie."

"Yeah, we are," Gracie said with more conviction than she felt. "Mebbe we should ask after

Charlie, not Uncle Alf? Most people push their own barrows, or got 'orses."

Minnie Maude brightened. "Yeah. Ye're right." She squared her shoulders and lengthened her stride, marching across the icy cobbles toward a thin man with a lantern jaw who was busy mending a broken window, replacing the small pane of glass, smiling as he worked, as if he knew a secret joke.

"Mister?" Minnie Maude jogged his elbow to attract his attention.

He looked at her, still smiling.

Gracie caught up and glanced at the window. The old pane he had removed had a neat hole in it, round as the moon.

"Wot's yer name?" Minnie Maude asked.

"They call me Paper John. Why?"

"Yer bin 'ere afore?" Minnie Maude watched him intently. "Like three days ago, mebbe? I'm lookin' fer where me uncle Alf were. 'E 'ad a cart, but wif a donkey, not an 'orse."

"Why?" The man was still smiling. "Yer lorst 'im?"

"I lorst Charlie, 'e's the donkey," Minnie Maude explained. "Uncle Alf's dead."

The smile vanished. "Sorry ter 'ear that."

" 'E's a rag an' bone man," Minnie Maude went on. "Least 'e were."

"This is Jimmy Quick's patch," the man told her.

"I know. Uncle Alf did it fer 'im that day."

"I remember. 'E stopped and spoke ter me."

Minnie Maude's eyes opened wide, and she blinked to stop the tears. "Did 'e? Wot'd 'e say?"

" 'E were singin' some daft song about Spillikins and Dinah an' a cup o' cold poison, an' 'e taught me the words of it. Said 'e'd teach me the rest if I got 'im a drink at the Rat and Parrot. I went, but 'e never turned up. I reckoned as 'e di'n't know the rest, but I s'pose 'e were dead, poor devil."

Minnie Maude gulped. " 'E knew 'em. 'E used

ter sing it all, an' 'Ol' Uncle Tom Cobley' an' all too," she said.

"Oh, I know that one." He hummed a few bars, and then a few more.

Gracie found her throat tight too, and was angry with herself for letting it get in the way of asking the right questions. "Did 'e say as 'e'd picked up anyfink special?" she interrupted.

The man looked at her curiously. "Like wot?"

"Like anyfink," she said sharply. "Summink wot weren't just rags an' old clothes and bits o' fur or lace, an' ol' shoes or bones and stuff."

"Jus' things wot nobody wanted," the man said gently. "Bit o' china wot was nice, four cups an' saucers, a teapot wi' no lid. 'E must a just 'ad a fit, fallen off. Could 'appen ter anyone. 'E weren't no chicken."

"Yeah. I'm sure," Gracie replied, but she wouldn't have been if she had not seen the blood and the scratches at the stable, and if Stan had not been so angry. It was the prickle of evil in the air, not the facts that she could make sense of to someone else. " 'E were killed."

The man pursed his lips. "Well 'e were fine when I saw 'im, an' 'e di'n't say nuffink." He hesitated for a moment. " 'E were late, though, fer this end o' the way. Jimmy Quick's round 'ere a couple of hours sooner . . . at least."

"Yer sure?" Gracie asked, puzzled. She did not know if it meant anything, but they had so little to grasp on to that everything could matter.

"Course I'm sure," the man replied. "Mebbe 'e were lorst. 'E was goin' that way." He pointed. "Or 'e forgot summink an' went back on 'isself, like."

Gracie thanked him, and she and Minnie Maude continued along the way that he had indicated.

"Wot's 'e mean?" Minnie Maude said with a frown.

"I dunno," Gracie admitted, but she was worried. It was beginning to sound wrong already.

Why would anyone change the way he went to pick up old things that people put out, even good things? She tried to keep the anxiety out of her face, but when she glanced sideways at Minnie Maude, she saw the reflection of the same fear in her pinched expression, and the tightness of her shoulders under the shawl.

A couple of hundred yards farther on they found a girl selling ham sandwiches. She looked tired and cold, and Gracie felt faintly guilty that they had no intention of buying from her, not that they wouldn't have liked to. The bread looked fresh and crusty, but they had no money to spare for such things.

"D'yer know Jimmy Quick?" Gracie asked her politely.

The girl gave a shrug and a smile. "Course I do. Comes by 'ere reg'lar. Why?"

"Cos me Uncle Alf did it fer 'im three days back," Minnie Maude put in. "Did yer see 'im?" She forced a smile. "Wot's yer name?"

"Florrie," the girl replied. "Ol' geezer wi' white 'air all flying on top o' 'is 'ead?"

Minnie Maude smiled, then puckered her lower lip quickly to stop herself from crying. "Yeah, that's 'im."

" 'E made me laugh. 'E told me a funny story. Silly, it were, but I in't laughed that 'ard fer ages." She shook her head.

"Was 'e goin' this way?" Gracie pointed back the way they had come. "Or that way?" she turned forward again.

Florrie considered. "That way," she said finally, pointing east.

"Are yer certain?" Gracie said to Florrie. "That'd mean 'e were goin' backward ter the way Jimmy Quick'd do it. Yer real certain?"

Florrie was puzzled. "Yeah. 'E come that way, an' 'e went up there. I watched 'im go, cos 'e made me laugh, an' 'e were singin'. I were singin' along wif 'im. A man wif a long coat got sharp wif me cos

I weren't payin' 'im no 'eed when 'e asked me fer a sandwich."

"A man wif a long coat?" Minnie Maude said instantly. "Did 'e go after Uncle Alf?"

Florrie shook her head. "No. 'E went the other way."

"We'll 'ave a sandwich," Gracie said quickly, feeling rash and expansive. She fished for a coin and passed it over. Florrie gave her the sandwich, and Gracie took it and carefully tore it in half, giving the other piece to Minnie Maude, who took it and ate it so fast it seemed to disappear from her hands.

It was much more difficult to find the next person who had seen Alf and Charlie. Twice they got lost, and they were still west of Cannon Street. The wind was getting colder, slicing down the alleys with an edge, like knives on the skin. It found every piece of bare face or neck, no matter how carefully you wound a shawl or how tightly you pulled it. The wind stung the eyes and made them water, spilling tears onto your cheeks, then freezing them.

Horses and carts passed, with hooves sharp on the ice and harnesses jingling. Shop windows were yellow-bright as the light faded early in the afternoon. It was just about the shortest day, and the lowering sky made it even grayer.

Everyone seemed busy about their own business, buying and selling to get ready for Christmas. People were talking about geese, puddings, red candles and berries, spices and wine or ale, happy things, once-a-year sort of things to celebrate. There were no church bells ringing now, but Gracie could hear them in her mind: wild, joyful—there for everyone, rich or poor, freezing or warm beside a fire.

They just weren't there for Alf, or for lost donkeys by themselves in the rain, and hungry.

It was late and heavy with dusk when they found the roasted-chestnut stand, on Lower

Chapman Street. The brazier was gleaming red and warm, sending out the smell of coals burning.

" 'E'd a stopped 'ere," Minnie Maude said with certainty. "If 'e'd a come this way. 'E loved chestnuts."

Gracie loved them too, but she had already spent too much. Still, they had to ask.

"Please, mister," Gracie said, going right up to the stand. "Did yer see the rag an' bone man three days ago, 'oo weren't Jimmy Quick? 'E were Uncle Alf, an' 'e did Jimmy's round for 'im that day, cos Jimmy asked 'im ter. D'yer see 'im?"

" 'Im wot died? Yeah, I saw 'im. Why?" The man's face reflected a sudden sadness, even in the waning light.

" 'E were me uncle," Minnie Maude told him. "I wanna know w'ere 'e died, so I can put a flower there."

The man shook his head. "I know w'ere 'e died, but I'd leave it alone, if I was you."

Suddenly Gracie's attention was keen again.

"Why? D'yer reckon summink 'appened ter 'im? We gotta know, cos we gotta find Charlie."

The man's eyebrows rose. " 'Oo's Charlie?"

" 'Is donkey," Minnie Maude said quickly. " 'E's missin', an' 'e's all by 'isself. 'E's lorst."

The man looked at her, puzzled.

"We can't 'elp Uncle Alf," Gracie explained. "But we can find Charlie. Please, mister, wot did Uncle Alf say to yer? Did 'e say anyfink special?"

"Me name's Cob." Wordlessly he passed them each a hot freshly cooked chestnut. They both thanked him and ate before he could change his mind.

Then Gracie realized what he had said. Cob! Was this the same Cob that Dora and Jimmy Quick had spoken of that Alf had shown the golden casket to? She swallowed the chestnut and took a deep breath.

"Did 'e tell yer wot 'e'd picked up?" she asked, trying to sound as if it didn't matter all that much.

"Yeah," Cob replied, eating a chestnut himself. " 'E said as 'e'd got summink real special. Beautiful, it were, a box made o' gold." He shrugged. "Course it were likely brass, but all carved, an' 'e said it were a beautiful shape, like it were made to 'old summink precious. I told 'im no one puts out summink like that. It'd be cheap brass, maybe over tin, but 'e said it were quality. Wouldn't be shifted. Stubborn as a mule, 'e were."

Minnie Maude's face was alight. " 'E 'ad it? Yer sure?"

"Course I'm sure. 'E showed it to me. Why? Weren't it wif 'im when 'e were found?"

"No. 'E were all alone in the street. No cart, no Charlie."

Cob's face pinched with sadness. "Poor ol' Alf."

" 'E di'n't steal it. It were put out." Minnie Maude looked at Cob accusingly.

Gracie's mind was on something more important, and that didn't fit in with any sense. "But 'oo knew as 'e 'ad it?" she asked, looking gravely at Cob. 'E wouldn't tell no one, would 'e? Did you say summink?"

Cob flushed. "Course I di'n't! Not till after 'e were dead, an' Stan come around askin'. I told 'im cos 'e 'ad a right, same as you." He addressed this last to Minnie Maude.

"Yer told 'im as Uncle Alf got this box?" Gracie persisted.

"Di'n't I jus' say that?" he demanded.

Gracie looked at him more carefully. He wasn't really lying, but he wasn't telling the truth either, at least not all of it.

" 'Oo else?" she said quietly, pulling her mouth into a thin line. "Someone else 'ad ter know."

Cob shrugged. "There were a tall, thin feller, wif a long nose come by, asked, casual like, after Jimmy Quick. I told 'im it wasn't Jimmy that day, an' 'e di'n't ask no more. Di'n't say nuffink about a gold box."

"Thin an' wot else?" Gracie asked. "Why were 'e lookin' fer Jimmy Quick?"

" 'Ow'd I know? 'E weren't a friend o' Jimmy's, cos 'e were a proper toff. Spoke like 'e 'ad a plum in 'is mouth, all very proper, but under it yer could tell 'e were mad as a wet cat, 'e were. Reckon as Jimmy 'ad some trouble comin'."

"Jimmy, not Uncle Alf?" Gracie persisted.

"That's wot I said. Yer got cloth ears, girl?"

"Wot else was 'e like?"

"Told yer, tall an' thin, wif a long nose, an' a coat that flapped like 'e were some great bird tryin' ter take off inter the air. An' eyes like evil 'oles in the back of 'his skull.

Gracie thanked him as politely as she could, and grasping Minnie Maude by the hand, half-dragged her away along the darkening street.

"Were 'e the one?" Minnie Maude asked breathlessly. "The toff wi' the long nose? Did 'e kill Uncle Alf?"

"Mebbe." Gracie stepped over the freezing gutter, still pulling Minnie Maude after her.

It was almost fully dark now, and the lamplighter had already been through. The elegant flat-sided lamps glowed like malevolent eyes in the growing mist. Footsteps clattered and then were instantly lost. There was hardly anyone else around. Gracie imagined them all sitting in little rooms, each with a fire, however small, and dreaming of Christmas. For women it might be flowers, or chocolates, or even a nice handkerchief, a new shawl. For men it would be whisky, or if they were very lucky, new boots. For children it would be sweets and homemade toys.

They stopped at the next corner, looking at the street sign, trying to remember if the shape of the letters was familiar. Gracie wasn't even sure anymore if they were going east or west. One day she was going to know what the letters meant, every one of them, so she could read anything at all, even in a book.

It was then that they heard the footsteps, light and easy, as if whoever made them could walk for miles without ever getting tired. And they were not very far away. Gracie froze. She was thinking of the man Cob had described, tall, with a long nose. That was silly. Why would he be there now? If he had killed Uncle Alf, he must already have the golden casket.

Nevertheless she turned around to stare, and saw the long figure in the gloom as it passed under one of the lamps. For a moment she saw quite clearly the flapping coat, just as Cob had said.

Minnie Maude saw the figure too, and stifled a shriek, clasping her hand over her mouth.

As one, they fled, boots loud on the stones, slipping and clattering, jumping over gutters, swerving around the corner into an even darker alley, then stumbling over loose cobbles, colliding with each other and lurching forward, going faster again.

The alley was a mistake. Gracie crashed into an old man sleeping in a doorway, and he lashed out at her, sending her reeling off balance and all but falling over. Only Minnie Maude's quick grasp saved her from cracking herself on the pavement.

Still the footsteps were there behind them.

The two girls burst out into the open street again, lamps now seeming almost like daylight, in spite of the thickening swathes of fog. The posts looked like elongated women with shining heads and scarves of mist trailing around their shoulders. The light shone on the wet humps of the cobbles and the flat ice of the gutters. Dark unswept manure lay in the middle of the road.

Gracie grabbed at Minnie Maude's hand and started running again. Any direction would do. She had no idea where she was. It could not be very far from Commercial Road now, and from there she could find Whitechapel Road, and Brick Lane. But this part was so unfamiliar it could have been the other end of London.

Somewhere down on the river a foghorn let out its mournful cry, as if it were even more lost than they were. Gracie's breath hurt in her chest, but the footsteps were still there behind them. Minnie Maude was frightened. Gracie could feel it in the desperate grasp of her thin, icy fingers.

"C'mon," Gracie said, trying to sound encouraging. "We gotta get out o' the light. This way." She made it sound as if she knew where she was going, and charged across the road into the opening of a stable yard. She could hear shifting hooves behind doors, and she could smell hay and the warm animal odor of horses.

"We could stay 'ere," Minnie Maude whispered, her voice wavering. "It'd be warm. 'Orses won't 'urt yer. 'E wouldn't find us in 'ere."

For a moment it sounded like a good idea, safe, no more running. But they were trapped. Once inside a stable, there would be no way to get out past him. Still, even if he looked, he wouldn't see them in the dark, not if they got into the hay.

"Yeah . . . ," she said slowly.

Minnie Maude gripped her hand tighter. As one they turned to tiptoe across the yard toward the nearest stable door.

"Next one," Gracie directed, just so as not to be obvious, in case the man did come in there. Although what difference would one door along make, if he really did look for them?

Then there he was, in the entrance, the street-lamp behind him making him look like a black cutout figure without a face. He was tall, and his chin was impossibly long, way down his chest.

"Gracie . . ." His voice was deep and hollow. "Gracie Phipps!"

She couldn't even squeak, let alone reply.

He walked toward them.

Minnie Maude was hanging on to Gracie's hand hard enough to hurt, and she was jammed so close to her side that she was almost standing on top of Gracie's boots.

The man stopped in front of them. "Gracie," he

said gently. "I told you not to go after the casket. It's dangerous. Now do you believe me?"

"Mr. . . . Mr. Balthasar?" Gracie said huskily. "Yer . . . di'n't 'alf scare me."

"Good! Now perhaps you will do as you are told, and leave this business alone. Is it not sufficient for you that poor Alf is dead? You want to join him?"

Gracie said nothing.

Mr. Balthasar turned his attention to Minnie Maude. "You must be Minnie Maude Mudway, Alf's niece. You are looking for your donkey?"

Minnie Maude nodded, still pressing herself as close to Gracie as she could.

"There is no reason to believe he is harmed," he said gently. "Donkeys are sensible beasts and useful. Someone will find him. But where will he go if in the meantime this man who murdered Alf has killed you as well?"

Gracie stared at him. There was not the slightest flicker of humor in his face. She gulped. "We'll go 'ome," she promised solemnly.

"And stay there?" he insisted.

"Yeah . . . 'ceptin' we don' know w'ere 'ome is. I'm gonna learn ter read one day, but I can't do it yet."

He nodded. "Very good. Everyone should read. There is a whole magical world waiting for you, people to meet and places to go, flights of the mind and the heart you can't even imagine. But you've got to stay alive and grow up to do that. Make me a promise—you'll go home and stay there!"

"I promise," Gracie said gravely.

"Good." He turned to Minnie Maude. "And you too."

She nodded, her eyes fixed on his face. "I will."

"Then I'll take you home. Come on."

$\mathcal{T}$ he next day was just like any other, except that Gracie had more jobs to do than ever, and her gran was busy trying to make a Christmas for them all. Gracie got up early, before anyone else was awake, and crept into the kitchen, where she cleared out the stove, and tipped the ashes on the path outside to help people from slipping on the hard, pale ice. Then she laid the wood and lit the new fire. She balanced the sticks carefully and blew a little on them to help the fire take. First she put the tiniest pieces of coal on and made sure they took as well. The small flames licked up hungrily, and she put on more. It was alarming how quickly they were eaten and gone. Lots of things went quickly. One moment they were there, and the next time you looked, they weren't.

It would be Christmas in two days. There would be bells, and singing, lots of lights, people would wear their best clothes, and ribbons, eat the best food, be nice to one another, laugh a lot. Then the next day it would all be over, until another year.

The good things ought to stay; someone ought

to make them stay. The dresses and the food didn't matter, but the laughing did, and you didn't wear the bells out by ringing them. Did happiness wear out? Maybe things didn't taste so sweet if you had them all the time?

She was still thinking about that when Spike and Finn came stumbling in, half-awake. Reluctantly they washed in the bucket of water in the corner. Then, wet-haired and blinking, they sat down to the porridge, which was now hot. They left plates almost clean enough to put away again.

By the end of the afternoon, Gracie's chores were finished, and her mind kept going back to Minnie Maude. She had to be worrying about Charlie. What kind of a Christmas would it be for her if he was not found? If they went looking around the streets, just for Charlie, not asking about Uncle Alf, or the golden casket, would that be breaking their promise to Mr. Balthasar? It was the casket the toff wanted, not a donkey who really wasn't any use to him.

She did not sleep very well, tossing and turning beside her gran, listening to the wind whistling through the broken slates. She woke up in the morning tired and still more worried. It was Christmas Eve. There was no reason why she should not at least go and see Minnie Maude and ask her how she felt about things.

She made sure the whole house was tidy, the stove backed up, the flatirons put where they could cool without scorching anything. Then she wrapped herself in her heaviest shawl, with a lighter one underneath, and set out in the hard sleet-edged wind to find Minnie Maude. Although she knew what Minnie Maude would say. Donkeys had hair all over them, of course, but it wouldn't be much comfort in this weather. When she had wet hair, she froze!

Bertha was in her kitchen, her face red, and she looked flustered. She opened the door, and as soon as she saw Gracie on the step, she put out a hand and all but hauled her inside, slamming the door shut after her.

"Yer seen Minnie Maude?" she said angrily. "Where'd that stupid little thing go now?"

Gracie's heart beat wildly, and her breath almost choked her. There was something badly wrong; she hardly dared even think how wrong. She could see that the red marks on Bertha's face were weals from someone's hand striking her, and Bertha held one shoulder higher than the other, as if even when she wasn't thinking of it, it hurt her and she needed to protect it.

"I in't seen Minnie Maude since two days ago," Gracie answered, looking straight into Bertha's red-rimmed eyes. "We said as we wouldn't look anymore ter see wot 'appened to 'er uncle Alf, cos it were too dangerous—" She knew immediately that she had made a mistake, but there was no way to take it back. Bertha would know the moment she lied. If you weren't used to lying, and the lie mattered, it always showed in your face.

"Wot d'yer mean, dangerous?" Bertha asked,

her voice dipping very low. "Wot yer bin askin'? Wot've yer done?"

Something near the truth was best. "Where 'e were killed," Gracie replied. "Minnie Maude wanted ter put a flower there." She kept her eyes steady, trying not to blink too much. Bertha was watching her like a cat studying a mouse hole in the wall.

"Well, it don't matter," Bertha said at last. "Put it anywhere. Alf won't care. 'E's dead an' gorn. You tell 'er that. She don't listen ter me."

"I will," Gracie promised. "Where is she?"

Bertha's face was white beneath the red weals. "I thought as she'd gorn ter sleep in the stable, but she in't there. Then I thought as she'd mebbe gorn fer you."

"No! In't seen 'er since two days ago." Gracie heard her own voice touched with panic. "When d'yer see 'er terday?"

Bertha's voice was husky. "I di'n't see 'er terday."

A dark fear fluttered in the pit of Gracie's stomach. "Wot did she take a miff about? Were it summink ter do wi' Jimmy Quick, or the chestnut man?"

"It were summink ter do wif 'er always meddlin'," Bertha replied. "Stan lost 'is temper wif 'er summink awful. I were afeared 'e were gonna 'it 'er, but 'e di'n't. 'E jus' lit out, white as paper, swearin' witless, an' next thing I know, she were gorn too."

Gracie was too frightened to be angry, and she could see that beneath Bertha's arrogance and self-defense, she was frightened also. There was no point in asking her for help.

"Well, if she in't 'ere, no point in me lookin'," Gracie said, as if that were some kind of reason.

Bertha opened her mouth as if to answer, then closed it again without speaking.

Gracie turned and left, walking away across the yard and out into the street again. She did not go back toward her own home; there was nothing to see that way. Where would Minnie Maude go, and, more urgently, why? What was Stan so angry about, and why was Bertha afraid? If Bertha were just afraid that Minnie Maude had been gone all night, she would have been looking for her herself, not standing around working in the kitchen.

Gracie's step slowed because she had no idea where to begin. One thing she was certain of as the wind sliced through her shawl, chilling her body, was that no one stayed out all night in this weather without a reason so harsh it overrode all sense of safety or comfort. Minnie Maude was looking for Charlie, but she must have had some idea where he was, or else there was something she was so frightened of at home that staying out alone in the icy streets was better.

What Gracie needed was to work out what Minnie Maude would have done. Something pretty urgent, or she would have waited until today, and told Gracie about it. Unless she'd thought Gracie had given up!

She stood at the curb watching the water flecked with ice running high over the gutters, as the wind whined in the eaves of the houses in the street behind her. The hooves of a horse pulling a dray clattered on the stones, wheels rumbling behind it.

Gracie had promised Mr. Balthasar not to ask any more questions about Uncle Alf's death. Minnie Maude knew that Gracie had meant it. Minnie Maude wouldn't have gone to look for Gracie; she would have gone off on her own. But where? Jimmy Quick wasn't going to tell them anything more. Even Minnie Maude wouldn't wander around the streets hoping to catch sight of Charlie. She must have gone somewhere in particular.

Which way had they gone before? Gracie looked left, and right. Minnie Maude would have gone down to the Whitechapel High Street and over into Commercial Road, for sure, then into the narrower roads with people's names, on either side of Cannon Street. If Gracie could just find those streets, she would know where to begin.

She set off briskly, and was on the far side of the goods yard before she was lost.

She looked to the left and couldn't remember any of the shop fronts or houses. She turned the other way. There was a broken gutter sticking out in the shape of a dogleg that she thought she'd seen before. That was as good a reason as any for making a decision. She went that way.

She passed an ironmonger's window with all sorts of strange tools in it, things she couldn't imagine using in a kitchen. She couldn't have been there before. If she'd seen those things, she would have remembered them.

Where on earth had Minnie Maude gone? It was Gracie's fault. She should have known better than to trust her. Minnie Maude loved that wretched donkey as much as if it had been a person, maybe more! Donkeys didn't lie to you, or swear at you, or tell you off, say that you were useless or lazy or cost the earth to keep. Maybe Charlie even loved her back. Maybe he was always happy to see her?

All right, so maybe Minnie Maude wasn't stupid to be loyal to a friend, just daft to go off without telling anyone. Except who cared anyway? Bertha? Maybe, but she didn't act like it. She was more scared than anything—maybe of Stan?

There was no point in standing there in a strange street. Gracie set off again, briskly this time. At least she would get a bit warmer. A few hot chestnuts would be a good thing right then. Maybe Minnie Maude had gone back to Cob, to see if he knew anything more? Or if not Cob, then maybe Paper John, although he hadn't said anything very helpful.

Who else might she have looked for? The crossing sweeper, Monday? Without realizing it she was walking more slowly, thinking hard, grasping for memory, and reasons. What had Minnie

Maude done that had made Stan so angry? Or was he just scared too, but would rather get angry than admit being scared? If Alf really had been killed by someone over the golden casket, then could Stan know something about it?

How did he know what Minnie Maude had been doing? She had said something, she must have. But what? Had she told him something, or asked him? Or he'd said something, and she had remembered . . . or understood—but what?

Gracie stopped in the shelter of a high building with a jutting wall. There was no point in going any farther until she worked things out. She might be going in the wrong direction, and would only have to go all the way back. The wind was harder and there were occasional pellets of ice in it. Her fingers were numb. She leaned against the wall where an uneven door frame offered her a little shelter.

Why had Minnie Maude gone? She must have had a reason, something that had happened—or something that had suddenly made sense to her. If Stan had said something, what could that be? How would he know anything about it anyway?

Or was it some meaning she'd put together, and then she'd seen a pattern?

A hawker pushed his barrow across the street, wheels bumping in the gutter, the wind in his face.

Think! Gracie said to herself angrily. *You were there all the time. Everything Minnie Maude heard, so did you! What did she understand all of a sudden?*

She was shaking with the cold, but there was no point in walking anywhere if she didn't know where to go. And the other thing, if she was really thinking as hard as she could, she wouldn't be noticing where she was, and she'd get even more lost. That wouldn't help Minnie Maude or Charlie, or anyone else.

Where had she and Minnie Maude been when they'd followed Jimmy Quick's route? What had they seen, or heard? They'd spoken to Monday, the crossing sweeper on Cannon Street. She tried to recall everything he had said. None of it seemed to matter much. Certainly it wouldn't have sent Minnie Maude out of the house, breaking her promise, and on a bitter night with ice on the wind.

Then there'd been Florrie, the peddler; and Paper John. Then there was Cob, the chestnut seller. He'd said a lot. He was the one who'd seen the toff, and Alf had actually told him about the golden casket.

But the more Gracie thought about it all, the less did she see anything in it that she hadn't seen two days before. Nobody had spoken of anything suspicious. It was exactly the same route, though backward, as Jimmy Quick always took—the same streets, the same people saw him. He had even started at about the same time. She could remember most of the streets, only not necessarily in the same order. But Alf would have had it right, because it made sense. One street led into another. There was only one way to go.

She tried again to remember exactly what everyone had said. She closed her eyes and hunched her shoulders, wrapping her shawl even more tightly around herself, and pictured the roasted-chestnut man. He was the only one who had seen Alf after he'd had the casket. Cob had looked worried, but not really downright frightened. She could see it in her mind's eye, the way he'd stood, his expression, the way he had waved his arms to show which way the man he'd called the toff had come . . . except that he had been coming the way Alf was going, not the way he had just passed! That made no sense.

She tried it again, but with Cob waving the other way. Except that he couldn't have. He was standing next to the brazier, about the length of his forearm from it. If he had waved that arm, he would have hit the brazier, and very likely burned himself. He might even have knocked it over. So it couldn't be right.

She tried turning him around, but that didn't work either. He had definitely pointed the way Alf was still going, not where he had been. She recited the order of the streets Jimmy had told them. Then she tried to say them backward, and got them jumbled up.

There was only one answer—Alf had done them the other way around. He had started at the end, and worked back to the beginning. The same circle—but backward.

Had someone counted on him doing it the same way as always? They would have expected him to be at a certain place at a certain time. The casket had been left for someone else. Alf had taken it without realizing it was important. Whoever it was—the toff—had gone after him to get it back, and by that time Alf had decided he wanted to keep it. Perhaps there had been a fight, and Alf had been killed because he wouldn't give it up?

Then why take Charlie? Why take the cart? And whose blood had it been on the stable floor?

It was getting colder. There was no answer that made sense of everything. The only things that seemed certain were that Alf was dead, Charlie and the cart were missing—and Alf had taken Jimmy Quick's route backward, being just about everywhere when nobody expected him.

Oh, and there was one other thing—the casket was missing, too. If it hadn't been, then the toff wouldn't still be looking for it. And worst of all, Minnie Maude was missing now too. That was Gracie's fault. She had left her alone when she knew how much the little girl cared. If she'd thought about it, instead of how tired and cold she was, and how much help her gran needed, then she would have seen ahead. She'd have gone to Minnie Maude's earlier, in time to stop her from wandering off and then getting taken by the toff.

Well, Gracie would just have to find her now. There wasn't anything else she could possibly do. She had to use her brains and think.

There was more traffic in the street, people coming and going, carts, wagons, drays, even one or two hansoms. Who had left the casket out with the old things for the rag and bone man, not expecting him to come by for hours? Why would anybody do that? For somebody else to pick up, of course. That was the only thing that made sense.

Who would that be? The toff, naturally. But who'd left it? And why? If you wanted somebody to have something, wouldn't you just give it to them? Leaving it on the side of the street was daft!

Unless you couldn't wait? Or you didn't want to be seen? Or somebody was chasing you?

Only, Alf had come along instead, and too soon. Perhaps it had been hidden inside an old piece of carpet, or inside a coal scuttle, or something like that. Then no one else would even have known it was there.

What did Alf do with it? He'd had it when he'd stopped for hot chestnuts, because Cob had seen it. Then where had Alf gone? He couldn't have had it when he was killed, or whoever killed him would have taken it away—wouldn't they?

Maybe it wasn't the toff who'd killed him?

But if somebody else had, then why? Because of the casket—it was the only thing special and different. Then what on earth was inside it that was worth so much—and was so dangerous? It must have been something very powerful, but not good. Good things, a real gift from the Wise Men for Jesus, wouldn't make people kill one another like this. Alf was dead, Bertha was frightened stiff, and Stan was angry enough to hit her in the face, probably because he was scared as well.

And Gracie was so afraid for Minnie Maude that she felt a kind of sickness in her stomach and a cold, hard knot inside her, making it difficult to breathe. Every time she thought she had made sense out of it all, it slipped away. She needed to get help. But from who? None of the people she knew would even understand, and they all had their own griefs and worries to deal with. They would just say that Minnie Maude had run off, and she'd come back when she got cold or hungry enough. They'd tell Gracie to mind her own business, look after Spike and Finn, and do as her gran told her.

She looked up and down the street as it grew busier. People hurried along the pavement, heads bent, the rain and sleet pounding. Many of the people were carrying parcels. Were they presents for Christmas? Nice food—cakes and puddings? There'd be holly with red berries, and ivy, maybe mistletoe, and ribbons, of course.

There was one person she could ask. He'd be very angry, because she had promised to stop asking questions, but this was different. Minnie Maude was gone. He could be angry later.

She straightened up, turned back the way she had come, and started walking into the wind. It stung her face and seemed to cut right through her shawl as if her shawl had been made of paper, but she knew where she was going.

*M*r. Balthasar looked at her grimly. His dark face, with its long, curved nose, was set in lines of deep unhappiness.

Gracie swallowed, but the lump in her throat remained.

"Will yer please 'elp me, mister, cos I dunno 'oo else ter ask. I think Minnie Maude's in trouble."

"Yes," he agreed quickly. "I think she probably is. You look frozen, child." He touched her shoulder with his thin hand. "And wet through. I will find you something dry, and a cup of tea." He started to move away.

"There in't time!" she said urgently, panic rising in her voice. Warm and dry would be wonderful, but not till Minnie Maude was found.

"Yes, there is," he replied steadily. "A dry shawl will take no time at all, and you can tell me everything you know while the kettle is boiling. I shall close the shop so we will not be disturbed. Come with me."

He locked the door and turned around a little sign on it so people would not knock, then he found her a wonderful red embroidered shawl and wrapped it around her, instead of her own wringing-wet one. Then, while she sat on a stool and watched him, he pulled the kettle onto the top of the big black stove, and cut bread to make toast.

"Tell me," he commanded her. "Tell me everything you have done since you last spoke to me, where you went and what you have discovered."

"First day I 'elped me gran, then terday I went ter see Minnie Maude, an' she weren't at 'ome," Gracie began. "'Er aunt Bertha tol' me as she'd gorn out, after Stan shouted at 'er. 'E were real mad, an' Bertha were scared. There were red marks on 'er face where 'e'd 'it 'er." It sounded silly now that she told him, because she hadn't actually seen it and couldn't explain any of her feelings. People did hit each other, and it didn't have to mean much.

He did not point out any of that. Turning over the toast to brown the other side, he asked her how Bertha sounded, what she looked like.

"And so you went looking for Minnie Maude?" he said when she had finished. "Where?"

"I thought as she must 'ave remembered summink," she replied, breathing in the smell of the crisp toast. "Or understood summink wot didn't make no sense two days ago."

"I see." He took the toast off and spread a little butter on it, then jam with big black fruit in it. He put it on a plate, cut it in half, and passed it to her.

"Is that all for me?" Then she could have kicked herself for her bad manners. She wanted to push the plate away again, but that would have been rude too, and the toast was making her mouth water.

"Of course it is," he replied. "I shall be hurt if

you don't eat it. The tea will be ready in a minute. What did she realize, Gracie?"

"Well, we knew Alf went the wrong way," she said, picking up a piece of the toast and biting into it. It was wonderful, crisp, and the jam was sweet. She couldn't help herself from swallowing it and taking another bite.

"The wrong way?" he prompted.

She answered with her mouth full. "Jimmy Quick always goes round 'is streets in one way. Uncle Alf went the other way. 'E started at the end, an' did it backward, so 'e were always everywhere at the wrong time." She leaned forward eagerly. "That were when 'e picked up the casket, nobody were expectin' 'im even ter be there. It were put fer someone else!"

"I see." The kettle started to whistle with steam, and Balthasar stood up and made the tea. "Do you know why he did that?"

"No." Now she wondered why she didn't know, and she felt stupid for not thinking of it.

"I shall inquire," he replied. "If something caused him to, such as a carriage accident blocking a road, or a dray spilling its load so he could not get past, that might be different from his deliberately choosing the other way around. Presumably this man, the toff, went to collect the casket, and found that it was gone. How did he know that the rag and bone man had taken it?" He put up his hand. "No, no need to answer that— because all the stuff for the rag and bone collection was gone. But he caught up with poor Alf—so if Alf was going the wrong way round, how did the toff know that?" He brought the teapot to the table and poured a large mug full for her. He passed the mug across, his black eyes studying her face.

"I dunno," she said unhappily. "D'yer think as 'e worked it out? I mean that Alf 'ad gone the wrong way round?"

"How did he know it was Alf, and not Jimmy Quick, as usual?" Balthasar asked. "No, I rather think he was waiting and watching, and he saw what happened."

"Then why di'n't 'e go after 'im straigh'away?" Gracie asked reasonably. "In fact, if the casket were left there for 'im, why di'n't 'e take it before Alf even got there? That don't make no sense."

Balthasar frowned, biting his lip. "It would if he did not wish to be seen. Whoever left it there for him would know what was in it, and that it was both valuable and dangerous. It might be that the toff could not afford to have anyone see him with it."

Gracie gulped. "Wot were in it?"

"I don't know, but I imagine something like opium."

"Wozzat?" she asked.

"A powder that gives people insane dreams of pleasure," he replied. "And when they wake up, it is all gone, and so they have to have more, to get the dreams back again. Sometimes they will pay a great price, even kill other people, to get it. But it is not something to be proud of, in fact very much the opposite. If the toff is an addict, which means that he can no longer do without it, then he will do anything to come by it—but he will take great care that none of his friends know."

For a moment she forgot the toast and jam.

"Someone put it there for him, in the casket," Balthasar went on. "And he waited out of sight, to dart out and pick it up when they were gone. Only this time Alf came by before he could do that. Continue with your tea, Gracie. We have business to do when we are finished."

"We 'ave?" But she obeyed and reached for the mug.

"We have a little more thinking to do first." He smiled bleakly. "I would tell you to go home, because I believe this will be dangerous, but I do not trust that you would obey. I would rather have you with me, where I can see you, than following after me and I don't know where you are and cannot protect you. But you must promise to do as I say, or we may both be in great danger, and Minnie Maude even more so."

"I promise," she agreed instantly, her heart pounding, her mouth dry.

"Good. Now let us consider what else we know, or may deduce."

"Wot?"

He half-concealed a smile. "I apologize—what we may work out as being true, because of what we already know. Would you like another piece of toast? There is sufficient time. Before we do anything, we must be certain that we have considered it all, and weighed every possibility. Do you not agree?"

"Yeah. An' . . . an' I'd like another piece o' toast, if you please."

"Certainly." He stood up quite solemnly and cut two more slices of bread and placed them before the open door of the oven. "Now, let us consider what else has happened, and what it means. Alf had the casket at the time he spoke to the chestnut man—Cob, I believe you called him? If we know the route that Mr. Quick normally took, then we know what the reverse of it would be, with some amendments for traffic. Hence we know where Alf is most likely to have gone next. And we know where his body was found."

"Yeah, but it don't fit in, cos 'oo's blood is it on the stable floor? An' 'oo fought there an' bashed up the wall? An' why'd 'e take Charlie an' the cart as well?" She drew in her breath. "An' if 'e killed Alf an' took the casket, wot's 'e still looking for? That's stupid. If I done summink wrong, I don't go makin' a noise all over the place. I keep me 'ead down." She colored with shame as she said it, but right then the truth was more important than pride.

"You have several good points, Gracie," Mr. Balthasar agreed. "All of which we need to address." He turned the toast over and filled her mug with fresh, hot tea.

"Thank you," she acknowledged. The heat was

spreading through her now, and she looked forward to more toast and jam. She began to realize just how cold she had been.

"I think it is clear," he continued, sitting down again, "that the toff does not have the casket, or at the very least, he does not have whatever was inside it. If he did, he would not only, as you say, keep his head down, he would be enjoying the illicit pleasures of his purchase."

She did not know what "illicit" meant, but she could guess.

"So where is it, then? 'Oo's got it?" she asked.

"I think we must assume that Alf did something with it between speaking to Cob and meeting whoever killed him presumably the toff. Unless, of course, it was not the toff who killed him but someone else. Although to me that seems rather to be complicating things. We already have one unknown person . . ."

"We 'ave? 'Oo?"

"Whoever passed that way just before Alf, and

left the casket," he replied. "Have you any idea who that could be?"

She felt his eyes on her, as if he could will her to come up with an answer. She wished she could be what he expected of her, and even now she wished she could think of something that really would help Minnie Maude.

"Is it someone 'oo knew where Charlie's stable is?" she asked, wondering if it was silly even as she said it. "Cos somebody 'ad a fight there. We saw the marks, an' the blood on the floor."

"Indeed. And do you know if it was there before Alf went out with Charlie the day he was killed?" he asked with interest.

She saw what he was thinking. "Yer mean if it weren't Alf or Charlie, then it 'ad ter be ter do wi' the casket?"

"I was assuming that, yes. What does this Stan do for a living, Gracie? Do you know?"

"Yeah. 'E's a cabbie . . ."

Mr. Balthasar nodded slowly.

"An' 'e's mad, an' scared," she added eagerly. "D'yer think Minnie Maude worked that out too?" Her eyes filled with tears at the thought of what violence might have happened to Minnie Maude, if Stan were the one who had left the casket for the toff.

"I think we had better finish our tea and go and speak to Cob," Balthasar answered, rising to his feet again. "Come."

"I gotta get me own shawl, please?" she said reluctantly. Compared with the thick red one, hers was plain, and wet.

"I will return it to you later," he replied. "This one will keep you warm in the meantime. Come. Now that we have so many clues, we must make all the haste we can." And he strode across the wooden floor and flung open the back door, grasping for a large black cape and swinging it around his shoulders as he went.

Outside in the street he allowed her to lead the way, keeping up with her easily because his legs were twice the length of hers. They did not speak, simply meeting eyes as they came to a curb, watching for traffic, then continuing.

They found Cob on his corner, the brazier giving off a warmth she could feel even when she was six or seven feet away.

Balthasar stood in front of Cob, half a head taller and looking alarmingly large in his black cape. He seemed very strange, very different, and several people stared at him nervously as they passed, increasing their pace a little.

"Good afternoon, Mr. Cob," Balthasar said gravely. "I must speak to you about a very terrible matter. I require absolute honesty in your answers, or the outcome may be even worse. Do you understand me?"

Cob looked taken aback. "I dunno yer, sir, an' I dunno nothin' terrible. I don't think as I can 'elp yer." He glanced at Gracie, then away again.

"I don't know whether you will, Mr. Cob. You may have black reasons of your own for keeping such secrets," Balthasar answered him. "But I believe that you can."

"I don't 'ave no—" Cob began.

Balthasar held up his hand, commanding silence. "It concerns the murder of a man you know as Alf, and the abduction of Minnie Maude Mudway."

Cob paled.

Balthasar nodded. "I see you understand me perfectly. When Alf left you, on the day he died, which way did he go?"

Cob pointed south.

"Indeed. And it was two streets farther than that where someone caught up with him and did him to death. Somewhere in that distance Alf gave the casket to somebody. Who lives or works along those streets, Mr. Cob, that Alf would know? A pawnshop, perhaps? A public house? An old friend? To whom would such a man give a golden casket?"

Cob looked increasingly uncomfortable. "I dunno!" he protested. " 'E di'n't tell me!"

"How long after Alf spoke to you did this gaunt gentleman come by?"

Cob moved his weight from one foot to the other. "Jus' . . . jus' a few moments."

"Was he on foot?"

"Course 'e were," Cob said derisively. "Yer don't go 'untin' after someone in a carriage!"

"Hunting," Balthasar tasted the word. "Of course you don't. You don't want witnesses if you catch him, now, do you?"

Cob realized that he had fallen into a trap. "I di'n't know 'e were gonna kill 'im!" he said indignantly, but his face was pink and his eyes too fixed in their stare.

Gracie knew he was lying. She had seen exactly that look on Spike's face when he had pinched food from the cupboard.

"Yer mean yer thought as the toff, all angry an' swearin', were one of 'is friends?" she said witheringly. "Knows a lot o' rag an' bone men, does 'e?"

"Listen, missy . . . ," Cob began angrily.

Balthasar stepped forward, half-shielding Gracie. He looked surprisingly menacing, and Cob shrank back.

"I think you would be a great deal wiser to give an honest answer," Balthasar said in a careful, warning voice. "How long after Alf was here did the toff come and ask you about him?"

Cob drew in breath to protest again, then surrendered. " 'Bout five minutes, I reckon, give or take. Wot diff'rence does it make now?"

"Thank you," Balthasar replied, and taking Gracie by the arm, he started off along the street again.

"Wot diff'rence does it make?" Gracie repeated Cob's question.

"Five minutes is quite a long time," he replied. "I do not think he would have run. That would draw too much attention to himself. People would remember him. But a man walking briskly can still cover quite a distance in that time. Alf would be going slowly, because he would be keeping an eye out for anything to pick up."

"Then why di'n't 'e catch up wif Alf sooner?" Gracie asked.

"I think because Alf stopped somewhere," Balthasar answered. "Somewhere where he left the casket, which is why he didn't have it when the toff killed him. And that, of course, is why the toff also took Charlie and the cart, to search it more carefully in private. He could hardly do it in the middle of the street, and with poor Alf's dead body beside him." He stopped speaking suddenly, and seemed to lapse into deep thought, although he did not slacken his pace.

Gracie waited, running a step or two every now and then to keep up.

"Gracie!" he said suddenly. "If you were to kill a rag and bone man, in the street, albeit a quiet one, perhaps a small alley, and you wished to take away the man's cart in order to search it, what would you do to avoid drawing attention to yourself and having everybody know what you had done?"

She knew she had to think and give him a sensible answer. She had to try not to think of Minnie Maude and the trouble she was in; it only sent her mind into a panic. Panic was no help at all.

"Cos I di'n't want nobody to look at me?" she pressed, seeking for time.

"I don't care if they look," he corrected. "I don't want them to see."

"Wot?" Then suddenly she had an idea. "Nobody sees rag an' bone men, less they want summink. I'd put 'is 'at on an' drive the cart meself, so they'd think I was 'im!"

"Magnificent!" Balthasar said jubilantly. "That is precisely what a quick-thinking and desperate man would do! In fact, it is not necessarily true that he was killed where his body was found. That too could have been carried a short way at least, and left somewhere to mislead any inquiry. Yes, that is truly a great piece of imaginative detection, Gracie."

Gracie glowed with momentary pride, until she

thought of Minnie Maude again. Then it vanished. "'As 'e got Minnie Maude?" she asked,
afraid of the answer.

"I don't know, but we will get her back. If he
took her, it is because he still doesn't have the casket, so he will not harm her until he does. We
must find it first."

"Well, if the toff don't 'ave it, then Alf must a
given it ter someone else between Cob an' wher-
ever 'e were killed."

"Indeed. And we must find out where that is. It
is unfortunate that we know so little about Alf,
and his likes and dislikes. Otherwise we might
have a better idea where to begin. Perhaps we
should assume that he is like most men—looking
for comfort rather than adventure, someone to be
gentle with him rather than to challenge him. Tell
me, Gracie, what did Minnie Maude say to you
about him? Why did she like him so much? Think
carefully. It is important."

She understood, so she did not answer quickly,

knowing her response would dictate where they would begin to look, and it might make the difference in terms of finding Minnie Maude in time to save her. It was silly to think Minnie Maude couldn't be hurt. Alf was dead—and they knew the toff was out there. She could well believe that the powder he was addicted to had driven him mad to the point where he had tasted evil, and now could not rid himself of it.

"'E were funny," she said, measuring her words and still skipping the odd step to keep up with him. "'E made 'er laugh. 'E liked 'orses an' dogs, an' donkeys, o' course. An' 'ot chestnuts."

"And ale?"

"Cider." She struggled to recall exactly what Minnie Maude had said. "An' good pickle wif 'am."

"I see. A man of taste. What else? Did she ever speak of his friends, other than Jimmy Quick? Tell me about Bertha."

"I think as Bertha is scared."

"She may well have reason to be. Who is she

scared of, do you think? Stan? Someone else? Or
just of being cold and hungry?"

She thought for a few moments. "Stan . . . I
think." She thought back further, into her own
earlier years, to when her father was alive. She
remembered standing in the kitchen and hearing
her mother's voice frightened and pleading. "Not
scared 'e'd 'it 'er, scared o' wot 'e might do that'd
get 'em all in trouble," she amended aloud.

"And Bertha is frightened and tired and a little
short of temper, as she has much cause to be?"

"Yeah . . ."

"Come, Gracie. We must hurry, I think." He
grasped her hand and started to stride forward so
quickly that she had to run to keep up with him as
he swung around the corner and into a narrower
street, just off Anthony Street—the way Jimmy
Quick's route would have taken them. They were
still two hundred yards at least from where Alf's
body had been found. Balthasar looked one way,
then the other, seeming to study the bleak fronts

of the buildings, the narrow doorways, the stains of soot and smoke and leaking gutters.

"Wot are yer lookin' fer?" she asked.

"I am looking for whatever Alf was seeking when he came here," Balthasar replied. "There was something, someone, with whom he wanted to share this casket he had found. Who was it?"

Gracie studied the narrow street as well. There was no pavement on one side, and barely a couple of feet of uneven stones on the other. Yet narrower alleys that led into yards invited no one. The houses had smeared windows, some already cracked, and recessed doorways in which the destitute huddled to stay out of the rain.

"It don't look like nowhere I'd want ter be," she said miserably.

"Nor I," Balthasar agreed. "But we do not know who lives inside. We will have to ask. Distasteful, but necessary. Come."

They set out across the road and approached the old woman in the first doorway.

Later, they were more than halfway toward the arch and gate at the end of the road when they found something that seemed hopeful.

"Took yer long enough," a snaggletoothed man said, leaning sideways in the twelfth doorway. He regarded Gracie with disfavor. "I 'ope yer in't expectin' ter sell 'er? Couldn't get sixpence for that bag o' bones." He laughed at his own wit.

"You are quite right," Balthasar agreed. "She is all fire and brains, and no flesh at all. No good to customers of yours. I imagine they like warm and simple, and no answer back?"

The man looked nonplussed. "Right, an' all," he agreed slowly. "Then wot der yer want? Yer can't come in 'ere wif 'er. Put people off."

"I'm looking for my friend, Alf Mudway. Do you know him?"

"Wot if I do? Won't do me no good now, will it! 'E's dead. Yer wastin' yer time." The man stuck out his lantern jaw belligerently.

"I know he is dead," Balthasar replied. "And I

know he was killed here. I am interested that you know it too. I have friends to whom that will be of concern." He allowed it to hang in the air, as if it were a threat.

"I dunno nuffink about it!" the man retaliated.

"One of my friends," Balthasar said slowly, giving weight to each word, "is a tall man, and thin, as I am. But he is a little fairer of complexion, except for his eyes. He has eyes like holes in his head, as if the devil had poked his fingers into his skull, and left a vision of hell behind when he withdrew them."

The color in the man's face fled. "I already told 'im!" he said in a strangled voice. "Alf come in 'ere ter see Rose, an' 'e went out again. I di'n't see nuffink! I dunno wot 'e done nor wot 'e took! Nor the cabbie neither! I swear!"

"The cabbie?" Balthasar repeated. "Just possibly you are telling the truth. Describe him." It was an order.

" 'E were a cabbie, fer Gawd's sake! Cape on for the rain. Bowler 'at."

Gracie knew what Balthasar had told her, but she spoke anyway.

"Wot about 'is legs?" she challenged. She knocked her knees together and then apart again. "Could 'e catch a runaway pig?"

Balthasar stared at her.

"Not in a month o' Sundays," the man replied. "Bowlegged as a Queen Anne chair."

Balthasar took Gracie by the arm, his fingers holding her so hard she could not move without being hurt. "We will now see Rose," he stated.

The man started to refuse, then looked at Balthasar's face again and changed his mind.

The inside of the house was poorly lit, but surprisingly warm, and the smell was less horrible than Gracie had expected. They had been told that Rose's was the third room on the left.

"I'm sorry," Balthasar apologized to her. "This may be embarrassing for you, but it will not be safe to leave you outside."

"I don' care," Gracie said tartly. "We gotta find Minnie Maude."

"Quite." Unceremoniously Balthasar put his weight against the door and burst it open.

What met Gracie's eyes was nothing at all that she could have foreseen. What she had expected, after Balthasar's words, was some scene of lewdness such as she had accidentally witnessed in alleys before, men and women half-naked, touching parts of the body she knew should be private. She had never imagined that it would be a half-naked woman lying on the floor in a tangle of bedclothes, blood splashed on her arms and chest, staining the sheets, bruises all over her face and neck.

Balthasar said something in a language she had never heard before, and fell onto the floor on his knees beside the woman. His long brown fingers touched her neck and stilled, feeling for something, waiting.

"Is she dead?" Gracie said in a hoarse whisper.

"No," Balthasar answered softly. "But she has been badly hurt. Look around and see if you can find me any alcohol. If you can't, fetch me water."

Gracie was too horrified to move.

"Gracie! Do as I tell you!" Balthasar commanded.

Gracie tried to think where she should look. Where did people keep bottles of whisky or gin? Where it couldn't be seen. In the bottom of drawers, the back of cupboards, underneath other things, in bottles that looked like something else.

Balthasar had Rose sitting up, cradled against his arm, her eyelids fluttering as if she were going to awaken, when Gracie discovered the bottle in the bottom of the wardrobe, concealed under a long skirt. She uncorked the top and gave it to him.

He said nothing, but there was a flash of appreciation in his eyes that was worth more than words. Carefully he put the bottle to Rose's lips and tipped it until a little of the liquid went into her mouth. She coughed, half-choked, and then took in a shaky breath.

"Rose!" he said firmly. "Rose! Wake up. You're going to be all right. He's gone and no one is going to hurt you again. Now breathe in and out, slowly."

She did so, and opened her eyes. She must have known from his voice that he was not whoever had beaten her. He had a slight foreign accent, as if he came from somewhere very far away.

"Rose," he said gently. "Who did this to you, and why?"

She shook her head a little, then winced at the pain. "I dunno," she whispered.

"It is too late for lies," he insisted. "Why?"

"I dunno." Tears slid down her cheeks. "Some geezer just went mad an' . . ."

Gracie bent down in front of her, anger and fear welling up inside her. "Course yer know, yer stupid mare!" she said furiously. "If yer don't tell us about the casket, an' 'oo took it, Minnie

Maude's going ter be killed too, jus' like Alf, an' it'll be on yer 'ead. An' nobody's never gonna fergive yer! Now spit it out, before I twist yer nose off."

Balthasar opened his mouth, and then changed his mind and closed it again.

Rose stared in horror at Gracie.

Gracie put her hand out toward Rose's face, and Rose flinched.

"A' right!" she squawked. "It were a toff with mad eyes, like a bleedin' lunatic. Proper gent, spoke like 'e 'ad a mouth full of 'ot pertaters. 'E wanted the gold box wot Alf gave me, and when I couldn't give it to 'im, 'e beat the 'ell out o' me." She started to cry.

Gracie was overcome with pity. Rose looked awful, and must have been full of pain in just about every part of her. Balthasar had wound the end of a sheet around the worst bleeding, but even the sight of so much scarlet was frightening. But if the toff had Minnie Maude, then obviously he could just as easily do the same to her, or worse. And Alf was already dead.

"Why di'n't yer give 'im the box?" Gracie demanded, her voice sharp, not with anger but with fear. "Wot's in it worth bein' killed fer?"

"Cos I don't 'ave it, eedjit!" Rose snapped back at her. "Don't yer think I'd 'ave given 'im the bleedin' crown jools, if I'd 'ave 'ad them?"

Gracie was dismayed. "Then 'oo 'as?" she said hollowly.

"Stan. Cos them Chinamen came to 'is place and beat the bejesus out of 'im for the money. 'E came 'ere jus' before. I reckon the bastard knew that lunatic were be'ind 'im, an' 'e went out the back. Then a few minutes after, this other geezer came in the front an' started in on me as soon as I din' give 'im the box."

"That is not the complete truth," Balthasar said quietly. "It makes almost perfect sense. Clearly Alf gave you the box, just before he was killed. At the time, no one else knew that, but Stan worked it

163

out. I daresay he knew Alf well enough to be aware of his association with you, so it was only a matter of time before he came here. We may assume that the toff was aware of this also, but not where you were, and therefore he followed Stan."

" 'Ow'd 'e know about Stan?" Rose looked at him awkwardly. Her cheek where she had been struck was swelling up, and one eye was rapidly closing. In a day or two the bruises would look much worse.

Balthasar glanced at Gracie, then back to Rose. "I think we can deduce that Stan was the one who placed the casket and its contents on the road near where the toff was waiting for the opportunity to pick it up. He hid in order that whoever dropped off the box would not see him. His addiction is not something he would care to have widely known, or his association with such people. When his addiction is under control, I daresay he is a man of some substance, and possibly of repute, and would then look much like anyone else.

We are seeing him when he has been deprived of his drug and is half-insane for the need of it."

Gracie shivered involuntarily. It was a thing of such destructive force that the evil of it permeated the room. "If 'e were followin' Stan, Minnie Maude weren't wif 'im, were she?" She swung around and stared accusingly at Rose. "Well, were she?"

"No! 'E were by 'isself!"

Gracie looked at Balthasar, desperation swelling into panic inside her. "If the toff's got 'er, why'd 'e chase after Stan? Where is she now? Is she . . . dead?"

Balthasar did not lie to her. "I don't think so. All the toff wants is the casket. He needs what is inside it as a drowning man needs air. Minnie Maude is the one bargaining piece he has. He will return to get her before he goes to where he expects to find Stan, then he will offer a trade— Minnie Maude for the casket."

Gracie gulped. "And Stan'll give it to 'im, an' Minnie Maude'll be all right?"

"I hope so. But we must be there to make sure that he does, just in case he has it in mind to do otherwise." He looked at Rose. "We will send for a doctor for you." He took a coin out of his pocket. "Where would Stan go, Rose?"

She hesitated.

"Do you want this ended, or shall we all come back here again?" he asked.

"Oriental Street, down off Pennyfields, near Lime'ouse Station," she said, her eyes wide with fear. "There's a stable there . . . it's—"

"I know." Balthasar cut her off. He put the shiny coin into her hand. "Pay the doctor with this. If you choose to spend it other than on your well-being, or lack of it, it is your own fault. Take care!" He stood up and went to the door. "Come on, Gracie. We have no time to waste."

At the entrance he told the snaggletoothed man to send for a doctor, or he would risk losing good merchandise. Then, outside in the alley, Balthasar marched toward the larger road, swung to the right, and continued on at such a pace that Gracie had to run to keep up with him. At Commercial Road East he hailed a cab, climbed up into it, pulling her behind him, and ordered the driver to go toward Pennyfields, off the West India Dock Road, as fast as he could.

"'Ow can we catch up wif 'im?" Gracie asked breathlessly as she was being thrown around uncomfortably while the cab lurched over icy cobbles, veered around corners, and jolted forward again. She was pitched from one side to the other with nothing to hang on to. "'E must be ages ahead of us."

"Not necessarily," Balthasar insisted. "Stan will be ahead of us, certainly, but he does not know anyone is following him."

"But the toff'll catch up wif 'im long before we do!" She was almost pitched into his lap, and scrambled awkwardly to get back straight on her own seat again. If this was what hansoms were like usually, then she was very glad she didn't ride in them often. " 'E could kill 'im too, ter get the casket. Then wot'll 'appen ter Minnie Maude?"

"I don't think Stan will be so easy to kill," Balthasar answered grimly. "He must know what is in the casket, and be used to dealing with the kind of men who trade in opium, and who buy it. The toff will know that, which is why he will take Minnie Maude with him. Stan will have to see her alive before he passes over anything." He touched her arm gently. "At least until then, Minnie Maude will be safe. But that is why we must hurry. Stan is a very frightened man, and the toff is a very desperate one."

Gracie turned and looked out the window. The houses were strange to her. Long windows had cracks of bright yellow light behind them, curtains drawn against the moonlit sky. She could see nothing beyond, as if the windows were blind, closed up within themselves. Maybe everyone inside the houses was all together, drinking tea by the fire, and eating toast and jam.

"Where are we?" she asked a few minutes later.

"We are still on Commercial Road." He rapped on the front wall of the cab with his fist. "Turn left into Pennyfields, just before you get to the West India Docks Station. Halfway along it is Oriental Street. Now hurry!"

"Right you are, sir!" the cabby answered, and increased speed again.

Gracie looked out of the window again. There seemed to be traffic all around them, carriages, other cabs, a dray with huge horses with braided manes and lots of brass, a hearse, carts and wagons of all sorts. They were barely moving.

"We gotta go faster!" she said urgently, grasping Balthasar's arm. "We won't get there in time like this!"

"I agree. But don't panic. They are stuck just as we are. Come, we shall walk the rest of the way. It is not far now." He pushed the door open and climbed out, passing coins up to the startled driver. Then, grasping Gracie by the arm again, he set off, head forward, pushing his way through the crowds.

Gracie wanted to ask him if he was certain he knew where he was going, but the noise was a babble like a field full of geese, and he wouldn't have heard her. It was hard enough just to keep hold of him and not get torn away by the people bumping and jostling their way, arms full of bags and boxes. One fat man had a dead goose slung over his shoulder. Another man had his hat on askew and a crate of bottles in his arms. There was a hurdy-gurdy playing somewhere, and she could hear the snatches of music every now and then.

She lost count of how far they went. She felt banged and trodden on with every other step, but if they could just find Minnie Maude in time, the rest was of no importance at all.

Here in the crowd it was not so cold. There was no space for the wind to get up the energy to slice through your clothes, and the shawl Mr.

Balthasar had given her was much better than her own. Her boots were sodden, but perhaps it was as well that her feet were numb, so she couldn't feel it every time a stranger stepped on them.

She did not know how long it was before they were gasping in a side alley, as if washed up by a turbulent stream into an eddy by the bank.

"I believe we have not far to go now," Balthasar said with forced optimism.

She followed him along the dark alley, their footsteps suddenly louder as the crowd fell behind them. Ahead the cobbles looked humpbacked and uneven, the little light there was catching the ice, making it glisten. The doorways on either side were hollow, the dim shadows of sleeping people seeming more like rubbish than human forms. In a hideous moment, Gracie felt as if the sleepers were waiting for someone to collect them—someone who never came.

Ahead there was a sound of horses shifting

weight, hooves on stone, a sharp blowing out of breath. It was impossible to see anything clearly. Lights were as much a deception as a help, a shaft of yellow ending abruptly, a halo of light in the gathering mist, a beam that stabbed the dark and went nowhere.

"Tread softly," Balthasar whispered. "And don't speak again. We are here, and both Stan and the toff will be here soon, if they are not already. Please God, we are soon enough."

Gracie nodded, although she knew he could not see her. Together they crept forward. He was still holding on to her so hard she could not have stayed behind even if she had wanted to.

Foot by foot they crept across the open space, through the wide gates and into the stable yard. Still they could see only tiny pools of light, the edge of a door, a bale of hay with pieces sticking out of it raggedly, the black outline of a cab and the curve of one wheel. There was a brazier alight. Gracie could smell the burning and feel the warmth of it more than see it. A shadow moved near it, a man easing his position, turning nervously, craning to catch every sound. She had no idea if it was Stan or not.

Balthasar kept hard against the wall, half-hidden by a hanging harness, its irregular shape masking his and Gracie's beside him. The tightening grasp of his hand warned her to keep still.

Seconds ticked by. How long were they going to wait? Somewhere ten or twelve yards away a horse kicked against the wooden partition of its stall with a sudden, hollow sound, magnified by the silence and the cold.

Stan let out a cry of alarm and jerked around so violently that for a moment his face was lit by the coals of the brazier, his cheeks red, his eyes wide with fear.

Nothing else moved.

Gracie drew in her breath, and Balthasar's fingers tightened on her arm.

From the shadows at the entrance a figure materialized, long and lean, its face as gaunt as a skull, a top hat at a crazy angle over one side of the brow. Deep furrows ran from the nose around the wide mouth, and the eyes seemed white-rimmed in the eerie light as the brazier suddenly burned up in the draft.

Stan was rigid, like a stone figure. From the look on his face, the man in the doorway might have had death's scythe in his hands. But it was nothing so symbolic that stirred beside the figure's thin legs and the skirts of the man's black frock coat. It was Minnie Maude, her face ash-pale, her hair straggling in wet rats' tails onto her shoulders. He had hold of her by a rope around her neck.

Gracie felt the cold inside her grow and her own body tighten, as if she must do something, but she had no idea what. She felt Balthasar's grip on her arm so hard it brought tears prickling into her eyes. She pulled away, to warn him, and he loosened it immediately.

"You did not deliver my box," the toff said quietly, but his perfect diction and rasping voice filled the silence, echoing in the emptiness of the stable. Somewhere up in the loft there would be hay, straw, probably rats. "Give it to me now, and I will give you the girl. A simple exchange."

"I left it fer yer," Stan retorted with a naked fear one could almost smell. "In't up ter me ter 'old yer 'and while yer sneak out an' pick it up. In fact, yer'd prob'ly cut me throat fer seein' yer if I did."

"I would have preferred that we not meet," the toff agreed with a ghastly smile. His teeth were beautiful, but his mouth twisted with unnameable pains. "But you have made that impossible." He gave a quick tweak to the rope around Minnie Maude's neck. "I have something that belongs to you. I will trade it for what you have that belongs to me. Then we will part, and forget each other. I imagine the men who supply you, and pay you whatever pittance it is, are not happy with you."

Stan's breath wheezed in his throat, as though

the whole cage of his chest were too tight for him. "I in't got it!"

"Yes, you have! Those who supply it want their money, and I want what is in my box. You want the child." He made it a statement, but there was an edge of panic in his voice now, and his eyes were wild, darting from Stan to the shadows where the light from the lanterns flickered.

Gracie was motionless, afraid that even her blinking might somehow catch his attention.

"Yer've always 'idden," Stan argued. "Now I've seen yer, wot's ter say yer won't kill me, like yer killed Alf?"

The toff drew in a quick breath. "So you do have it. Good. This is a beginning. You are quite right. I will kill to get what I need. With regret, certainly, but without hesitation." He pulled Minnie Maude a little closer to him, using the rope around her neck. She looked very thin, very fragile. One hard yank could break the slender bones. The end of her life would be instantaneous.

Balthasar must have had the same conviction. He let go of Gracie's arm and stepped forward out of the shadows.

"Do not lie to the man, Stanley." He spoke quietly, as if he were merely giving advice. If he was afraid, there was nothing of it in his voice, or in the easy grace with which he stood. "Alf gave it to Rose, perhaps as a gift. He had no idea what was inside it, simply that it was pretty. When you realized where it was, you took it from her, as he"— he gestured toward the toff, "knew you would. He followed you and beat that information out of Rose. He will not pay the suppliers until he has his goods, as you well know, which is why you are afraid of them. They will surely hold you accountable, possibly they already have. I imagine it is your blood on your stable floor, which is why you are terrified now."

Stan was shaking, but he kept his eyes on the toff, never once turning to look at Balthasar behind him. "An' 'e'll kill me if I do," he said. " 'E di'n't never want ter be seen. I 'ave ter leave it where 'e can watch me put it, then go, so 'e can creep out an' get it in private, like. Only that damn' Alf did Jimmy Quick's route all arse about-face, an' took it before 'e could come out."

"Yes, I had deduced that," Balthasar answered.

A slight wind blew through the open doors, and the lantern light wavered again.

"Give it to me, or I'll kill the girl!" the toff said more sharply. His patience was paper-thin, the pain of need twisting inside him.

"Then you will have nothing to bargain with!" Balthasar snapped, his voice the crack of a whip. "Stanley has the box, and he will give it to you."

The toff's eyes shifted from one man to the other, hope and desperation equally balanced.

The silence was so intense that Gracie could hear the horses moving restlessly in the stalls at the far side of the partition, and somewhere up in the loft there was the scrabble of clawed feet.

They waited.

Gracie stared at Minnie Maude, willing her to trust, and stay still.

Stan's eyes were fixed on the toff. "If I give it yer, 'ow do I know yer'll let 'er go?"

"You know I'll kill her if you don't," the toff replied.

"Then yer'll never get it, an' yer can't live without it, can yer!" Stan was jeering now, had become ugly, derisive, as if that knowledge gave him some kind of mastery.

The toff's body was shaking, the skin of his face gray and sheened with sweat where the lantern light caught him. He took a step forward.

Stan wavered, then stood his ground.

Minnie Maude whimpered in terror. She knew the toff was mad with need, and she had no doubt he would kill her, perhaps by accident if not intentionally.

"Give it to him," Balthasar ordered. "It is of no use to you, except to sell. There is your market standing in front of you. If he kills Minnie Maude, you can never go home! Have you thought of that? You will be a fugitive for the rest of your life. Believe me, I will see to it."

Something in his tone drove into Stan's mind like a needle to the bone. His shoulders relaxed as if he had surrendered, and he turned away from the toff toward the nearest bale of straw. He pushed his hand into it in a hole no one else could see, and pulled out a metal box about eight inches long and four inches deep. Even in the dim and wavering light the gold gleamed on the finely wrought scrollwork, the small fretted inlays, and the elaborate clasp. Gracie had never seen anything so beautiful. If it wasn't a gift for the Christ child, it should have been.

The toff's eyes widened. Then he hurled himself at it, his hands out like claws, tearing at Stan, kicking, gouging, and butting at him with his head, top hat rolling away on the floor.

Stan let out a cry of fury, and his heavy arms circled the man, bright blood spurting from Stan's nose onto the man's pale hair. They rocked back and forth, gasping and grunting, both locked onto the golden casket.

Then with a bellow of rage Stan arched his back, lifted the toff right off his feet, whirled him sideways, and slammed him down again as hard as he could. There was a crack, like dry wood, and the toff lay perfectly still.

Very slowly Stan straightened up and turned not to Minnie Maude but to Balthasar. "I 'ad ter do it! You saw that, di'n't yer." It was a demand, not a question. " 'E were gonna kill us all." When Balthasar did not answer, Stan turned to Minnie Maude. " 'E'd a killed you, an' all, fer sure."

Minnie Maude ran past him, evading his outstretched arms, and threw herself at Gracie, clinging on to her so hard it hurt.

It was a pain Gracie welcomed. If it had not hurt, it might not have been real.

"Yer stupid little article!" she said to her savagely. "Why di'n't yer wait fer me?"

"Just wanted to find Charlie," Minnie Maude whispered.

"I 'ad ter!" Stan shouted.

"Possibly," Balthasar replied with chill. "Possibly not." He held out his hand. "You will give me the casket."

Stan's face hardened with suspicion. He looked at Balthasar, then at Gracie and Minnie Maude standing holding on to each other.

"Like that, is it? Give it ter you, or you'll kill both of 'em, eh? Or worse? Do wot yer bleedin' want ter. I don' need two little girls. Blood's on yer 'ands." There was almost a leer on his face. "I should a known that's wot you were. Thought for a moment you was after saving Minnie Maude. More fool me."

Could that really be what Balthasar had wanted all the time—the gold casket, and the poisonous dreams inside it?

Balthasar looked at Stan as if he had oozed up out of the gutter. "I will give the opium back to those who gave it to you," he replied icily. "To save your life—not because you deserve it, but it is still a life. I will tell them it was not your fault, you are incompetent, not dishonest. You would be well advised not to seek them out again. In fact, it would be to your advantage if they did not remember your name, or the place where you live."

Stan stood with his mouth open, halfway between a gape and a sneer.

"As for the casket," Balthasar continued, "I shall give that to Gracie and Minnie Maude. I think they have earned it, and its owner no longer has any use for it." He glanced down at the toff, his face gaunt, oddly vacant now, as if his tortured spirit had left it behind.

"If you go immediately," Balthasar went on, still speaking to Stan, "you may not be found to blame for this, and the police do not need to know that you were here. Nor do the gentlemen who deal in opium."

" 'Ow do I know I can trust yer?" Stan asked,

but the belligerence was gone from his face and he spoke quietly, as though he would have liked an answer he could cling on to, one to save his pride.

"You don't," Balthasar said simply. "But when the police do not trouble you, and you never see or hear from the opium dealers again, you will know then."

Stan gave him the casket.

Balthasar opened it very carefully, but there was no secret catch to it, no needles to prick or poison. Inside was a fine silk bag full of powder, which he took. He put it into the pocket on the inside of his coat. Then he examined the box carefully, blew away any suggestion of powder or dust from every part of it, and wiped it with his handkerchief. He held it out to Gracie.

"I know that all you wanted was to save Minnie Maude, but I think you have earned this. You and Minnie Maude will decide what is best to do with it. But it is very precious. Do not show it to people or they may take it, although it has nothing inside it now."

Gracie reached out slowly, afraid to touch it, afraid even more to hold it in her hands.

"Take it," he repeated.

She shook her head, putting the tip of one finger gently on the shining surface. It was smooth, and not really cold. "It shouldn't be fer me," she said huskily.

"What would you like to do with it?" he asked.

"When I first 'eard about it, I thought it were a present—cos it's Christmas. Yer know—like wot the Wise Men brought for Jesus."

"Gold for the king, because He is king of all of us," he agreed. "Frankincense because He is priest, and myrrh because He is the sacrifice that redeems all of us from the death of the soul. Is that what you would like to do with it?"

She nodded. "Yeah. But I don't know 'ow. An' it's empty."

"Christ will know what it cost you to get it," he

told her. "And it doesn't matter a great deal where you go. Christmas is everywhere. But I do know of a place where some people are holding a very special Christmas Eve party, with a nativity scene. I can't take you, because I have to get rid of this poison, back to the people who own it, before they find Stan and take their price in his blood. But I can show you the direction to go."

"Wot's that wot you said?"

"A nativity scene? It is people creating a little play, like the first Christmas all over again. It's very special, very holy. Come." He looked at Minnie Maude. "Are you able to come too? It has to be done tonight, because this is Christmas Eve. This is the night when it happened in the beginning and created a whole new age, an age of hope, and a new kind of love."

Minnie Maude nodded slowly, gripping on to Gracie's hand.

"Can you walk a little?" Balthasar asked anxiously. "I can get you a hansom cab to ride in, but you will still have to walk at the far end."

"I in't got no money fer an 'ansom," Gracie told him. "I could pay for an omnibus, if there is one, mebbe?"

"I shall pay for it, and tell him exactly where to go. But I think you had better wrap up the casket in the edge of your shawl. We do not want to draw people's attention to it."

She took the casket from him and obediently wound the end of the red shawl around it until the box was completely hidden. "I'll bring the shawl back to yer after Christmas," she promised.

"If you wish," he said solemnly. "And I shall return you your own one, clean and dry. But if you prefer this one, we can leave matters as they are."

It was a wonderful thought. This one was warmer, and far prettier. But it must also have been expensive. She resisted the temptation. "That wouldn't be fair."

"As you wish. Now come. It is late and there is no time to spare. In less than an hour it will be Christmas Day."

*T*he ride in the hansom did not seem so long this time. Minnie Maude sat very close to Gracie, and once or twice Gracie even thought she might be asleep. They rattled through the dark streets of the East End back through the heart of the city toward the West End and the nice houses. All the lamps were lit and the wind had blown away the earlier fog. Gracie could see wreaths of leaves on doors, lighted windows, carriages with patterns and writing on the doors. Horse brasses gleamed. There was a sound of jingling, laughter, and people calling out cheerfully. Somewhere voices were singing.

"I'll be back fer yer," the cabby said when he stopped. "It's that 'ouse there." He pointed. "Yer stay there till I come fer yer, you 'ear."

"Yes, sir." Gracie clasped the casket in one arm, and Minnie Maude's skinny little hand in the other. Normally she would not have dreamed of pushing her way into a grand house like this, but she had a present to give to Jesus, and Mr. Balthasar had told her that this was the place to do it.

She and Minnie Maude walked over the cobbles and into the stables at the back of the big houses. There were lots of people around, all wearing smart clothes, ladies with fur muffs and woolen cloaks, and gentlemen with curly fur collars on their coats. No one seemed to mind them coming in.

"Wot are they all doin' 'ere?" Minnie Maude whispered. "They're just standin' around out 'ere in the stable."

"I dunno," Gracie replied. "But Mr. Balthasar said it were 'ere, so it must be."

There was a slight noise behind them and a ripple of excitement. The group nearest the entrance moved apart to allow passage through, and in the next moment a man in a long robe appeared. It was very plain, like pictures Gracie had seen from the Bible. The man had curly hair all over the place, as if he had forgotten to comb it. He was smiling, and he had a brownish-gray donkey by the halter. It had long ears and a pale nose, and on its back rode a young woman with hair like polished chestnuts. She was smiling too, as if she knew something so wonderful she could hardly contain the happiness of it.

The people standing in the stable yard held up their lanterns, and they all cheered. The donkey stopped by the open stable door, and the man helped the young woman down. She was clearly with child and she moved a little awkwardly, but she turned to touch the donkey gently and thank it for carrying her.

Gracie watched as if seeing a miracle. She knew what was going to happen next, as though she had already seen it before. In a few minutes the bells would ring for midnight, and it would be Christmas. Then Jesus would be born. There would be angels in the sky, shepherds coming to worship, and Wise Men to bring gifts. Would it still be all right to give hers?

She gripped Minnie Maude's hand more tightly and felt her fingers respond.

Then the bells started, peal after peal, wild and joyous, the sound swirling out over the rooftops everywhere.

The stable doors opened, and the young woman sat in the straw with a baby in her arms, the man behind her. There were a couple of horses, who probably lived there, and the donkey.

Three men came from the back of the scullery doorway, dressed up like shepherds, carrying big staffs with curly tops. The bystanders were quiet, but they were all smiling and holding one anothers' hands.

Next came the three Wise Men, each dressed more gorgeously than the one before. They had robes of reds and blues and purples. One had a turban wound around his head, another a gold crown. They all knelt before the baby and laid gifts on the ground.

Minnie Maude poked Gracie in the side. "Yer gotter give ours!" she urged. "Quick, or it'll be too late."

"Ye're comin' too!" Gracie dragged her forward, unwrapping the gold casket as she went and holding it out in front of her. Even here, among all this wealth and splendor, it shone with a beauty unsurpassed.

Gracie stopped in front of the young woman. "Please, miss, we'd like ter give this to the Baby Jesus. It oughter be 'is." Without waiting for permission, she put it down on the straw in front of her, then looked up. "It in't got nuffink in it," she explained. "We in't got nothing good enough."

"It is perfect as it is," the young woman replied. She looked Gracie up and down, then looked at Minnie Maude, and her eyes filled with tears.

"Nothing could be more precious." She was about to add something more when the donkey came forward through the straw and pushed his nose against Minnie Maude, almost knocking her off balance.

She turned and stared at him, then flung her arms around him, burying her face in his neck.

"Charlie!" she sobbed. "Where yer bin, yer stupid thing? I 'unted all over fer yer! Don't yer never do that again!"

"I'm sorry," Gracie said to the young woman. "She thought 'e were lorst."

"Well, he's found again," the young woman replied gently. "Tonight we are all found again." She turned to the man. "Thomas, I think we should see that these two girls have something hot to eat, and to drink." Then she looked at the donkey and smiled. "Happy Christmas, Charlie."

ABOUT THE AUTHOR

ANNE PERRY is the bestselling author of two acclaimed series set in Victorian England: the William Monk novels, including *Execution Dock* and *Dark Assassin,* and the Charlotte and Thomas Pitt novels, including *Buckingham Palace Gardens* and *Long Spoon Lane.* She is also the author of the World War I novels *No Graves As Yet, Shoulder the Sky, Angels in the Gloom, At Some Disputed Barricade,* and *We Shall Not Sleep,* as well as seven holiday novels, most recently *A Christmas Promise.* Anne Perry lives in Scotland. Visit her website at www.anneperry.net.

ABOUT THE TYPE

This book was set in Century Schoolbook, a member of the Century family of typefaces. It was designed in the 1890s by Theodore Low DeVinne of the American Type Founders Company, in collaboration with Linn Boyd Benton. One of the earliest types designed for a specific purpose, the *Century* magazine, it maintains the economies of a narrower typeface while using stronger serifs and thickened verticals.